## ~ REVIEWS FOR CURING DOCTOR VINCENT ~

# The Good Doctor Trilogy

Curing Doctor Vincent
Surviving Doctor Vincent
(coming fall 2015)
Loving Doctor Vincent
(coming 2016)

# Good Doctor Short Stories

Tasting Paris

# CURING DOCTOR VINCENT

THE GOOD DOCTOR TRILOGY
BOOK 1

*All my best,*

# RENEA MASON

SECRET HUNGERS PUBLISHING

**Curing Doctor Vincent**
The Good Doctor Trilogy – Book One
Copyright © 2015 by Renea Mason. All rights reserved.
http://reneamason.com

Published by Secret Hungers Publishing
http://www.secrethungers.com

ISBN-13: 978-1507795804
ISBN-10: 1507795807

Cover Designed by Alchemy Book Covers
http://www.alchemybookcovers.com/
Edited by Nancy Cassidy at The Red Pen Coach
http://www.theredpencoach.com/
Print & E-Book Interior Layout by Ryan Fitzgerald
http://ryanjamesfitzgerald.ca

First eBook edition – January 5, 2015
First print edition – March 11, 2015
First audio book edition – May 28, 2015

Revision: August 2015

# ~ Dedication & Acknowledgement ~

This book is dedicated to the Mad Masons—the most wonderful group of friends and supporters an author can have! It takes a book this naughty to honor a group this nice.

To my fellow authors who have given me support, mentorship and advice on this journey.

As always, thank you to my wonderful family, who make it all possible.

I'd like to thank the ladies who worked so hard supplying beta-edits to help me breathe life into Doctor Vincent and who have continually showed their support—The Mad Masons beta-readers – Tiffany Dover, Lisa Errion, Elizabeth "the fabulous" Robbins, Ashley Bodette, Beckey White, Sky Tillery, Crissy Sutcliffe, Amy Habel, Nicole "hooker" Ulery, Robin Malone, Debbie Willis, Sharie Robinson, Libby Sinclair and Amanda Miller. This story wouldn't be the same without them!

# CURING DOCTOR VINCENT

## CHAPTER ONE

# GUEST

"**T**HIS CHANGE WILL MAKE A HUGE DIFFERENCE TO PHYSI-cians prescribing the medication. Are there any questions?" With a quick sigh, I placed the laser pointer on the table, crossed my arms and wiped the sweat from my palms. It should have been an easy presentation, not unlike the hundreds I had given before, but this one was different.

Seated less than three feet away, in his expensive, dark gray suit, black tie and silver cufflinks, sat Dr. Xavier Vincent—company icon and legend. It wasn't every day the man who developed the cure for your sister's cancer showed up unannounced. His unshakable stare caused butterflies to stir in my stomach.

"I have a question." The doctor sat forward, raising his hand.

I swallowed hard. "Yes, Dr. Vincent?" And to think, I had thought of patting myself on the back for holding it together. He wasn't supposed to be in the meeting. He really should have abstained from asking questions.

"How long did it take you to compile this research?" I couldn't read his expression, but that didn't undermine the intensity of it.

"About six months, Sir." I rolled the seam of my jacket between my fingers. So many things ran through my mind. I should have worn that dress I pulled from the hotel closet earlier that morning and discarded, instead of a drab brown blazer and pants. I should have gotten that stylish haircut and highlights last week, instead of sticking my auburn mane in a messy up-do. I shouldn't have eaten that cheesecake on Tuesday. Had I only known he'd be here, I would have changed everything.

"Are you happy with your job?" He folded his arms on the table and sat up straight.

It was an unfair question, especially given the audience. I wasn't happy with my job, but refused to disrespect him with a lie. "It's important work that needs to be done."

He reached for his aluminum tumbler, took a drink, and licked the water from his lips. "That's not what I asked."

Distracted by the sweeping of his tongue over his full lower lip, I forgot to engage the filter on my mouth. "I…I'm sorry. I find fulfillment in my work, Doctor. That's the best any of us can ask, isn't it really? I think true contentment impedes progress. Shouldn't we all strive for something more? Happiness leads to complacency. So no, my job doesn't make me happy, but as I said, it is important work."

Several gasps echoed through the room. The doctor raised an eyebrow, paused, and then stood. "Well…thank you for your honesty, Elaine. If no one else has anything more for her, we can call it day. It was great to meet everyone and you are all invited to dinner at the Cornerstone Bistro at six-thirty. I hope to see you there."

*Shit. How could I be so stupid?* My mouth got me into this mess. Some say the truth is best unspoken, but not for me. My convictions left me incapable of lying.

I started the shutdown process on my computer and opened my bag to tuck away my notebook. I wanted to crawl into a hole and die.

The room was a flurry of activity as everyone vied for the doctor's attention. I couldn't blame them; the man was intriguing. Dark hair, laced with only trace strands of gray, betrayed his youth. In magazines, his young age and good looks always contrasted his accomplishments, securing him celebrity status among his peers. I remember seeing him on the cover of the *Forbes Magazine – Fabulous under Forty* edition. He couldn't be that much older than me. In reality, the sharp angles of his face, and the light dusting of silver, gave him an air of sophistication beyond his years. It seemed unfair for a man with his beauty to also be gifted with such intelligence. Nature should be careful to balance such things. I had never thought of him in those terms before, but he was handsome beyond compare—untouchable, god-like even. And I'd just told him I hated my job.

It only took a moment to remind myself that this was a medical conference, not a singles bar. Besides, he wasn't even on the market, the ring on his finger spoke of his commitments. But God...he was gorgeous. And every time he folded his large hands during the meeting, I had to will myself not to shiver. He had such long fingers. What the hell was wrong with me?

"Elaine?"

I looked up from my bag and the notebook slipped from my fingers. His steel blue eyes and strong jaw line made him look like a model, not a man capable of curing cancer. I needed to focus on something else, like a list of companies to submit my resume to. I cleared my throat. "Yes...Doctor."

"You are coming to dinner."

"I hadn't planned on it. I'm not part of the team. Just a guest speaker." I bent to collect the notebook from the floor, but he beat me to it. Our uncoordinated approaches caused me to smack my head into his.

"Ouch… Oh, I am so sorry. Are you okay?" I rubbed the sore spot on my head.

He laughed. "I'm fine." He handed me the notebook.

Laughter was good. At least I hoped. I reached for the book, recognizing for the first time just how tall he was. I halted for a moment at the intoxicating scent of his cologne. He smelled like spiced-chocolate. "I don't know what's wrong with me, I'm not usually this nervous." But if I had to venture a guess, it was the combination of being ill prepared for his surprise attendance and my increasingly horny single status.

"I know."

I stopped fidgeting with my items and fixed him with a perplexing stare. "I'm sorry?" Great, now I was even more unsettled.

"I saw you at the convention in Kansas City last year. You were quite confident."

*Shit.* Of all the things he could have witnessed. Kansas City wasn't my finest moment.

"Look, that convention…it was…I mean—"

"You don't owe me an explanation." He reached over and closed the lid on my laptop and handed it to me.

"Thank you, but I don't want to hold you up from dinner." And I didn't want to rehash Kansas City, so I jumped on his easy out. The disappointment of presenting marketing data at conferences, rather than representing the company as their spokesperson, was reminder enough.

"It wasn't a question. You are coming to dinner."

I pulled the zipper closed on my bag and then brushed

the hair from my eyes, to be sure that I wasn't dreaming. "OK. Where is it? I'll meet you there." I wasn't accustomed to feeling so inadequate, or discombobulated. He set me on edge. My skin tingled with sexual attraction and I wanted to throw myself at his feet for saving my sister. Dr. Vincent was making one fine mess of me.

He crossed his arms and his eyes narrowed. "Where are you staying?"

"At the Marriot."

"Perfect. I'll meet you in the lobby at six. Is that enough time?"

"Ahhh…yes…but…"

"Good." He turned and strode to the doorway. "Oh and Elaine…I don't like being stood up." With that he walked away.

* * *

The lobby was crowded at dinnertime. The bustle of patrons strolling through the common area with luggage made it hard to navigate. When I turned the corner, I ran into the good doctor's chest.

He maintained his balance and clutched my upper arms, stopping me before I had the chance to topple him. "There you are."

I knew in that moment this was not a good idea. My thoughts regarding him were anything but professional. Even the slightest contact with him set me on fire.

"Elaine, are you okay?" He leaned down and stared into my eyes.

I smiled at him. "Yes. I'm fine. Just a bit distracted."

"By?"

I wouldn't lie to him, but there was no way I was giving him the detailed truth. "I've got a lot on my mind."

He returned my smile. "Well…let's go get you a drink. The restaurant is only a few blocks away." He motioned toward the exit.

Through the revolving door and down the uneven slate sidewalk, we walked side by side. I tucked my hands into the pockets of my wool coat. Chicago was chilly this time of year and the wind caused me to shiver.

"So when did you start working for Western?" He stopped in front of a building that resembled a tavern, but with a French flair. The amber lighting from inside spilled through the windows, turning the walk a golden hue. He opened the door and motioned for me to enter.

Voices, cheering and laughing, engulfed me, and I turned my head to respond to him over my shoulder. "Right out of college. So it's been a few years."

The feel of his widespread hand on the small of my back, chased away the bite of the Chicago night.

He approached the host podium and a man with gray hair and a black apron said, "You with Western?"

The doctor, with his hand still on my back, answered the older man, "Yes."

The man scratched out something on a notepad and said, "Right this way."

At the table sat several of the meeting attendees. I didn't know anyone since I was only in town to present my research findings and was then headed back to New York. The doctor returned the many greetings he got from the team members with a quick wave.

I stopped breathing when his fingers brushed my neck. He hooked them around the collar of my coat and coaxed it down my shoulders. The doctor took two good strides in front of me and pulled out a chair. "Please, have a seat."

I did as he requested and he pushed in the chair for me. I willed myself to stop trying to find more in his actions than a sophisticated man being polite.

I took a deep breath and let out a long sigh as he disappeared with our coats. When he took a seat beside me, I wasn't sure if I'd survive the rest of the evening. He smelled so good. I knew it had to be my imagination, but I swore I could feel heat radiating from him. God…I needed to get laid.

The waiter, a man in his early twenties with red hair and a bright smile, approached the table. "Can I get you something to drink?"

The doctor's shoulder rubbed against mine, and then his hot breath brushed my ear. "What would you like to drink?"

Alcohol was not a good idea. The doctor wouldn't take kindly to being accosted by a horny, drunken co-worker and his wife would be even less happy.

I faced him and with one look into his eyes, I knew there could be no alcoholic drinks. "I'll have a water."

He raised an eyebrow and turned back to the waiter. "Two glasses of your best *pinot noir*."

It was my turn to give an incredulous glance.

Without hesitation, he responded, "Ms. Watkins, you have nearly given me a concussion, run me over in the lobby, and you have been distracted since our time in the conference room. Water is not what you need."

"Since when do doctors advise the use of alcohol?"

He leaned in closer. "When he thinks that the patient needs to forget her worries."

I huffed. "And I suppose arguing my point would get me nowhere."

"Are you allergic to alcohol?"

"No."

"On any medications that are contraindicated with alcohol use?"

"No."

"Then yes, you are quite correct. There is no use arguing."

The waiter returned with two glasses and a bottle. He poured a small amount of wine in one glass and presented it to the doctor. Dr. Vincent took a sip and nodded to the waiter, who then topped his glass and poured a second one, placing it in front of me before leaving.

The doctor lifted his glass and said, "To new and wonderful experiences."

I lifted my glass and it clinked as it touched the side of his. He raised his glass and stood. Over the sound of the big-screen TVs in every corner blaring the news broadcasts, various sports and music videos, the doctor made a toast. The twenty plus executives, salespeople and clinicians seated at the table, gave the doctor their full attention. "Thank you all for coming out tonight. But mostly, thanks to all of you who've worked so hard to get Lyenstat into the hands of the patients who so desperately needed it this past year. Even though I wanted to come here personally to thank all of you, my gratitude pales in comparison to the thanks that come from the thousands of brain cancer patients who now have a second chance. Everyone raise your glass…" He paused and waited until all hands were outstretched. "To health, happiness and all you truly desire." He lifted the glass to his lips and took a drink.

The clanging of glasses and chatter of joyful tidings surrounded the table. The doctor sat beside me.

"What do you desire, Elaine?"

I choked and started to cough.

He placed his hand on my back. "You OK?"

My shock turned to a laugh. "Yes, I'm fine." I took another drink to wash down the one that had stuck in my throat, sat the wine on the table and turned to him. "I desire…" God, I needed to be careful. "…To tell you how much I appreciate you."

His eyes grew wide and he rested his hand on my leg. Just a friendly gesture. *Stop reading more into it.*

"What exactly do you appreciate?" There was a teasing tone to his voice.

I smiled to myself, thinking of all the possible answers, but settled on, "That you saved my sister. She almost died of that horrid disease. But you…you finished the cure just in time. She was one of the first patients to take the drug. I can't thank you enough."

He clutched my hand in his. "Oh, Elaine, I don't know what to say, but I'm so thankful she's going to be OK. So thankful we got it to her in time." He looked away.

He still held my hand, but there was an obvious discomfort with my words.

"Look, I'm sorry. I didn't mean to make you uncomfortable."

He turned back. "Oh, I'm not. It's just my turn to be a bit distracted."

Out of the corner of my eye I caught an image that flashed across the TV screen and my stomach heaved. Shit. I had been traveling so often, the usual deluge of reporters banging on the door failed to alert me that it was time again. They hadn't caught up with me.

Before I could make a graceful exit, a bald-guy named Pete, who worked in physician sales, hollered from several seats away, "Hey, Elaine, isn't that your dad?"

*Fuck.* I grabbed the wine, took a large gulp and turned to the doctor. "Thank you so much for the drink, Doctor. It was very nice to meet you, but I have to go." I pushed my chair back, stood and paused, along with everyone else including the doctor, staring at the TV flashing images of my father. On the screen in the closed-captioning—*the country's most notorious serial killer continues his game of cat and mouse with detectives for the third straight year. In order to extend his stay on death row, Daniel Simon Watkins reveals one victim per year to authorities, on the anniversary of the murders. Tonight, police are still searching for the complete set of remains belonging to Margaret Marie Smith of Omaha Nebraska, Watkins' second victim, while family members of missing women from all over the world gather outside the New York State Penitentiary awaiting the name of his third. Police expect the "Basement Killer's" announcement this week.*

I didn't answer Pete, but turned and headed to the host podium. I spotted my coat on a rack nearby. I yanked it from the hanger and threaded one arm into the sleeve as I pushed the door open with my hip. The uneven sidewalk stifled my gait, but I wanted to get back to my room and lock the door. How could the man who gave me everything—the perfect childhood—become my biggest nightmare? He was the reason I could no longer have a career in public relations. No company wanted a PR rep with my kind of baggage. What was it with sales people and their nosey questions?

About three feet from the Marriot threshold, someone grabbed my arm. Fear sent a rush of adrenaline through me. Ready to fight, I screamed, "Let go of me."

"Elaine, it's me, Xavier, I think you've caused me enough bodily harm tonight. You don't need to try to kick my ass, too."

I took deep breaths, trying to calm myself. I couldn't face him.

Finally I managed, "Thanks for checking on me. I'm fine. You can head back."

He grabbed my hand and laced his fingers between mine and pulled me toward the entrance. He looped his arm around my waist and held me against his body as we navigated the revolving door.

Once inside he guided me to a corner of the lobby with a loveseat and a fireplace, away from the prying eyes of the hotel guests.

"Sit down. And note: it's not a request."

"Yes, Sir." I begrudgingly followed his instructions and hoped that appeasing him might end the discussion sooner. This is not how I wanted him to remember me.

"Look at me."

I stared at the fire. There was no way I could look at him.

He huffed. "Fine, have it your way." He turned so that his leg rested against mine. "You are not your father. Elaine, I was a practicing psychiatrist for many years."

I laughed, but the sound wasn't formed of humor. "So I finally get to meet the great Dr. Xavier Vincent and of all the embarrassing situations I could ever dream up, having him provide *pro bono* psychiatric help in a hotel lobby has to top them all. Reality really is more screwed up than fiction."

"That's not what I meant."

Another chuckle escaped and I turned to him. "Doctor, I really do appreciate your offer. It's very nice of you to come here to try to help me, but this is not the picture of me I wanted you to leave with. I'm not frail and I'm not weak. I am raw, and need to heal. As a shrink, you know that."

"How do you want me to see you?"

I inhaled, considering, then on an exhale I said, "A confident, decisive woman, who knows who she is. Not this mess you see tonight."

"Done."

I looked at him. "What?"

"That's exactly how I'll think of you. I always have."

I buried my head in my cupped hands, and I peered out to the world through my spread fingers, trying to not read more into his words than he could possibly mean.

His hand moved to rest on my knee. "Answer one question for me and I'll leave you for the night."

I sat up. "What do you want to know?"

"You said you know who you are. What I want to know is, who you are going to be? I mean after all, shouldn't we all strive for something more? Happiness only leads to complacency. At least that's what I was once told by a very wise colleague." He squeezed my leg, as he echoed back my words. "Tell me, Elaine, what more are you striving for, what are your desires?"

I took a deep breath and sat up. "That's hard to answer. It changes. Some days, it's simply to make it all go away. Others it's to keep focused on the good in things. Most times, it's being able to dream like I once did. I had a career, a future. Now I have a psychopathic dog and pony show that kills my ambitions every three hundred and sixty-five days. And times like tonight…"

He leaned in closer. "What about tonight?"

"Sometimes…I wish the distractions were enough."

"Perhaps you need bigger distractions."

I took a deep breath.

He patted my leg. "I'll keep my promise. Please, get some rest. I'm happy that we got to meet."

I chuckled, "Shouldn't that be my line?"

"Trust me, the honor is all mine." He stood. "I'm sure we will see each other again. It's a small world."

He turned and walked through the lobby. I watched him

until he disappeared behind a pillar. What a mess of a trip. All I hoped for was a good night sleep.

* * *

The next morning, I gathered my things and headed to the lobby to turn in my room key and catch the shuttle to the airport. The receptionist took the key. "How was your stay?"

I leaned my luggage against the counter. "Good."

"Oh, Ms. Watkins, I have a package for you. One moment…"

The tall, blond gentleman set a small package on the counter.

I figured I'd left something at the conference center. I tugged on the brown paper and it revealed another package, this one wrapped in gold foil. Careful not to tear the wrapping since it was so beautiful, I released the tape and slid a small box from inside.

The silver chest, adorned with tightly woven knotwork, was empty.

On the inside of the lid were the words,

> *"When Pandora opened the box and released evil onto the world, suffering became our burden. But in this story, most fail to recognize her gift—hope. For if the box can be emptied, it can once again be filled. Anything is possible if you believe hard enough. Lock away all that haunts you to find all you've ever hoped for."*

It wasn't signed. There was no author acknowledgement, but the gift could have only come from one person—Dr. Vincent.

## CHAPTER TWO
# FAVOR

"Elaine." Stanley Bergman smiled and waved me to a black leather chair in front of his desk. His suit was a drastic change from the toga he wore at the last frat party we'd attended. But he had the same wide smile and boyish features I remembered. "Stan…" I paused. "Or should I now call you Vice President, Sir?" It was strange to see him sitting behind the mahogany desk of one of largest pharmaceutical companies in the world—Chatum D. Western Labs.

He lowered his head, revealing the slightest tinges of premature gray in his dark strands of hair, but the move didn't hide his blush. "You saw me naked when they tied me to the light post during Rush Week. We're past formalities."

I laughed. "Yes, and if I remember, that cold night didn't do you any favors."

"Hey now, I had hoped you'd forgotten that part."

"Believe me, I tried." I smiled, and took the seat.

He fiddled with an envelope in his hand. "So… you're probably wondering why I asked you here, since you don't even work in my department." He folded his arms across the desk; cufflinks gleaming in the sunlight entering through the Venetian blinds.

"I am." I studied his deep brown eyes for any hint of anxiety. Why was I here? It had been months since my career died at that podium in Kansas City and it had been almost a week since my strange encounter with Dr. Vincent. I would never work in public relations again, but the marketing position they'd hidden me in since the incident had started to grow on me, even all the unappreciated staff presentations I was tasked with giving. I would hate to lose it. Was he leaving? Restructuring perhaps?

He took a long breath and his short, chestnut curls bounced when he sighed. Over his tented fingers he asked, "Have you done something different with your hair?"

"My hair?" Why would he ask about my hair? Whatever his issue, it couldn't be good. "I pulled it up today, but other than that, it's the same as it was in college—long and reddish-brown. What's going on, Stan?"

He turned the envelope end over end, and adjusted a notebook so that it covered the morning's newspaper on his desk. Before he obscured the headline, I read—*World's Most Prolific Serial Killer to Release Name of Victim Number Three.*

"Is that what this is concerning? Him?" I pointed to the paper. "You don't need to hide it. Do you honestly think I haven't seen it? Every year the media crawls out of the woodwork to chase me down and hash it all over again. I had to dodge them this morning, barely made it to my car."

"I can't even imagine what that's like." He gave me the look everyone always did—sympathy laced with morbid curiosity.

I crossed my arms, trying to hide my irritation. "You know what? Neither can I. It's been three years, and it still doesn't seem real. And the sad thing is I don't know how long it will go on. No one knows the real body count, but him."

I hadn't talked to Stan about it, but everyone knew the

story. It was something I avoided and foolishly thought everyone else would too. I don't think anyone can ever come to terms with the fact that his or her childhood was a farce—some kind of perversion of the perfect fairytale. The white house, the picket fence, two children, adoring parents... It all crumbled three years ago when the nightly news flashed the missing persons photo of Abigail Evans.

"It must be difficult."

I leaned toward him and fixed him with a penetrating stare. "Stan, difficult is your dog dying. Finding out your father is a serial killer...well...that's beyond difficult. I sacrificed my childhood for truth and justice...I'm lucky I'm sane."

He cleared his throat. "Do you still talk to him?"

"Who? My father? No, my childhood and my career were payment enough for the fantasy he gave me. I don't owe him anything else."

His brow furrowed. "Your career?"

"Come on Stan." I slammed my hands against the chair arms. " I have a degree in public relations from one of the most prestigious universities in this country yet the first time my father is brought up at a public event, the company sticks me in an office, never to be heard from again, except to regurgitate information to employees. You can't have a PR rep with my kind of baggage. I'm a distraction."

"Why do you stay?"

I took a deep breath. "He'll still be there for me to answer for no matter where I go. This company saved my sister's life. Without that cancer drug, she would be dead. She is the last thread I have to a normal life—the only person who can understand how I feel. And at least I'm doing some good, even if it is behind a desk, instead of representing Western to the public."

"Speaking of that..." He paused and rubbed his hands on his pants. "When you were in Chicago..."

Why did he seem so nervous?

"After the presentation you gave on adherence, I heard you spoke with Dr. Vincent. What happened?" He rubbed his jaw while maintaining eye contact.

I shifted in my seat, sitting forward. This was a line of questioning I didn't expect. "Nothing big. Why do you ask?"

"Nothing is small regarding Dr. Vincent. Come on, what happened?"

I raised an eyebrow. "He asked if I was happy with my job."

"And?"

"If you're worried I told him that the company relegated me to the dungeon, I didn't. I simply said that I had an important job." I shot him a suspicious glare. "Why? I was so nervous speaking to the man I could barely form words. I really wish someone would have tipped me off that he would be there." Stan didn't need to know about our private conversation, or the box. Besides, I wasn't one hundred percent certain it was from the doctor. I just had no other suspects.

"No one expected him to be there. That's the kind of man he is." He tapped the envelope against the desk again.

I wondered if Stan had developed a nervous tick. I didn't understand his behavior. Nothing I'd done warranted retribution. The experience had been much like meeting a rock star. My brain had pretty much checked out and I'd made a fool out of myself. The main thing I remembered about the good doctor was how good he smelled and... "Did I say something wrong? I swear, I didn't say anything about you or Western."

"OK." He sighed. "Dr. Vincent is very important around

here. He's the icon. Hell, since he discovered Lyenstat and revolutionized oncology research, no one even remembers who Chatum D. Western is, and he founded the damn company. Dr. Vincent might not directly manage anything, but don't think he doesn't call the shots."

"Of course. Vincent put Western on the Fortune 100 list. Trust me, I understand how important he is, beyond all the lives he saved." I resisted the urge to roll my eyes.

"Yes. And there are rumors that he is very volatile and decisive."

I gasped. "Shit. He didn't fire me, did he? Those stupid morons from sales. Son of—" I grasped the arms of the chair, squeezing, and tried to keep my cool. I might not have been happy with my banishment, but I needed the job. My father wasn't in a position to finish paying off my college loans.

"No, he didn't fire you. Settle down. What morons from sales?"

"That idiot from Kansas City. If he had just stuck to the talking points. Instead he brought up how it must have been terrible having a father like mine when I was growing up. Instead of agreeing, I told the truth. I said my childhood was as close to perfect as one could get and my father was loving and kind to me. I didn't know what he was doing on the side. He accused me of condoning my father's actions, and they removed me from the podium before I could set the record straight. Then *bam* I'm assigned to marketing research." I pulled at a thread on my shirt. "Then that Pete guy from Chicago…" I ran my hands along the seam of my skirt. "What the hell is going on? Please just say it. I can handle it." I held my breath. This couldn't be good.

Stanley cleared his throat. "Dr. Vincent has requested your presence."

"OK. That's surprising." I sat up straighter. "Where and when?"

He handed me an envelope. "You leave tonight."

"Tonight? Is he crazy? Where to?" I took the thick white rectangle from his outstretched hand. Testing the seal on the envelope with my thumb, I resisted the urge to tear into it like a kid on Christmas Day.

"Maybe so. But please, Elaine, don't screw this up. Whatever you do is going to be a reflection on me. Not only because he came to me, the VP assigned to his product operations, with his request, but I was the person who recommended you to Western in the first place."

"Gee, Stan, thanks for the vote of confidence." I glared at him.

"No, you don't understand. There are rumors about Dr. Vincent, and with your hotheaded temper..."

"My temper?" The heat flooding my cheeks made it difficult to deny his accusation. I shook my head. I took a strong stance in one meeting and now I was the stuff of legends. In my defense, it had been an ethical issue. But I had to admit when I picked my hill to die on, my demise was theatrical.

"Yes. You can be rather...opinionated."

The fact that he was right irritated me more. "What kind of rumors?"

"You know, eccentric genius with control issues and all that. He might ask you to walk his cat or something stupid. If he does, just suck it up and go with it. Dr. Vincent is the reason I'm Vice President."

"Well, if the guy promoted you, why are you so afraid?" I stared at the thick, white envelope in my hand. *Ms. Elaine Watkins* scrolled across the front in elegant script.

"He didn't promote me. He demanded the old VP be fired.

No reason. Just up and fired him. You've got to be careful. My three kids are depending on you."

"No pressure, huh?" I rolled my eyes.

"Elaine." It almost sounded like a whine.

"All right. I'll walk his cat with a smile on my face."

"Thank you." He relaxed in his seat.

I stood, stuffed the envelope under my arm and pointed at him. "You're going to owe me. I don't even like cats."

He laughed. "You have a cat."

"OK, I like cats, but they are a pain in the ass to walk."

Stan shook his head. "I'm sure Dr. Vincent will make it worth the effort."

It was my turn to laugh. "One can hope. Have you seen him? Plus he saved my sister, so a little feline sojourn won't kill me." I sighed. "This will be a good distraction from the drama surrounding my father. I hope I can keep myself together enough not to say something stupid." I smiled and glanced over my shoulder. "I'll call and let you know if you still have a job."

He stopped laughing. His brow furrowed. "That's not funny."

Making my exit, I pulled the door shut behind me.

I tore open the envelope.

Oh my God!

"Paris."

## CHAPTER THREE

# PARIS

THE CROWD OUTSIDE MY APARTMENT PARTED WITH RELUC- tance. Microphones appeared in front of my mouth, but just like every other year, silence was my only response to their constant inquiries. My father played the media just like he played his family and his victims, dragging out his death sentence for as long as possible with the promise of another victim's name on the anniversary of his yearly hunting trips. And to think, we assumed he hunted deer. I refused to play his game. Dr. Vincent's invitation couldn't have come at a better time.

Somewhere over the Atlantic Ocean, anxiety hit. What did I forget to pack? Did I pack enough underwear? And what was so important that I had to leave tonight? Sixteen hours later, after security, customs, and a delayed flight, the plane touched down in Paris.

After traversing the airport for a solid twenty minutes, I spotted a gentleman with salt and pepper hair dressed in a black uniform holding up a sign with 'Elaine Watkins' written in shaky script. I moved to stand in front of him.

"Elaine?" The thick French accent blended the two syllables of my name as though they were silk and satin. Such a beautiful language.

I nodded and he grabbed my bags.

His long legs made his stride swift, and I struggled to keep up. We stepped outside of baggage claim in front of a black stretch limo. He opened the door for me.

As my bottom slid across the smooth leather seat, I looked up into the older man's hazel eyes. "Where are we going?"

"*Pardon, mademoiselle. Je ne parle pas anglais,*" he said with a shake of his head, shrug of his shoulders and his hands spread.

I smiled. "Wonderful."

I prayed the ride would be short, but no such luck. As the scenery passed by and we navigated the narrow streets, the dancing lights of the city were a great distraction. Soon the city gave way to scenic French countryside; small farms with stone barns dotted the hills.

After more than an hour of driving, the sun had set, and in a faint glow of moonlight, we arrived at a large security gate. The driver pushed a button, muttered something in French and the gate opened. Another half-mile down a winding narrow road, a large structure emerged from the darkness.

The driver parked the car in front of a large, gothic, stone mansion. Beautiful gray stonework formed an elegant archway leading to iron and stained glass doors. Light from inside the building made the cut roses and ivy shimmer. The breathtaking architecture emanated history and wealth.

After opening my door, he waved me toward the stoop. I took his cue. He placed my bags on the walk beside me and returned to the car. I raised my fist to knock, but the door opened before I could. Dr. Vincent welcomed me instead of a butler. I never expected to see him outside of a work event.

His casual, yet expensive-looking, shirt and jeans made him look so approachable. Why was he here? A better question... why was I?

"Good evening, Elaine." He reached down, took my hand and kissed the back of it.

"Ah... Good evening...Dr. Vincent." I managed to smile through the nerves. This was very different than seeing him in his professional environment.

His furrowed brow drove away his welcoming expression. "Something wrong?"

I glanced around, taking in the hand cut stones that framed the threshold. The place must have cost a fortune. Pushing away my disconcertion, I replied, "No, nothing is wrong, Doctor."

He reached for my bags, but my hands beat him to the handles. This was the great Dr. Vincent. There was no way he was taking my bags.

He paused. "Elaine, may I take your baggage?"

"I'm OK. I'll just keep them with me until I leave for the hotel."

"Did you honestly think I would have you come all this way to sleep in a hotel? You are my guest and will stay here. Unless of course it's not to your—"

"No. No. It's perfect." But certainly unexpected.

He reached for my bags again and this time I released my grip and allowed him to take them. He smiled and nodded his approval. "I will only be a moment." He led us into the foyer.

As he walked away, I wound my arms around my chest and gazed up to see the massive cathedral ceiling decorated with shadows cast by the crystal chandelier. I took a deep breath, clenched and unclenched my hands. Not only was I standing in pure opulence, I was the guest of the gorgeous man who'd saved my sister's life. Much more than a celebrity, he was a saint.

It didn't take long before he appeared in the archway to the foyer.

He walked behind me, grabbed the shoulders of my coat and coaxed it down my arms. He spoke in soft tones, so close to my ear I felt his breath.

"Thank you for traveling all this way." The scent of spicy cologne soothed me—utter masculinity. Too wrapped up in my work and my father's nonsense, it had been years since I had been this close to a man. I couldn't afford to feel such things for the good doctor. Not only were there professional boundaries, he was married.

"If I hadn't made the trip, I would have never had the chance to see your magnificent home."

He smoothed my sleeves, his hands pausing for a moment on my biceps. He then stepped in front of me, draped my coat over his arm and motioned me forward. We made our way into the mahogany paneled great room.

"Well, thank you, but this is all my wife's doing. I have much simpler tastes."

The large room, with a roaring fire in the oversized stone hearth, was accented by a burgundy and cream color palette reminiscent of royalty. "Please, have a seat." He gestured to a large velvet brocade chair. He waited as I scooted back in the chair and straightened my skirt. "Do you prefer red or white?"

"Excuse me?" I was such a bundle of nerves. What the hell was I doing here? The situation was surreal.

"Wine, my dear. Do you prefer red or white? Or maybe I've read you wrong and you'd like something a little stronger." He smiled.

This was going to be the longest week of my life. I wasn't the nervous type, but the doctor evoked strange responses from me. "Red, please."

He winked. "That's what I thought." With my coat in hand, he headed back into the foyer.

The warmth of the fire felt wonderful, almost too soothing, as jet lag and exhaustion overcame me. It wouldn't look good if I fell asleep. The wine was not a good idea, but how could I refuse? The last time I tried to refuse him, I failed.

Moments later he returned with two glasses and handed one to me. "Here, my dear." He made sure I had a firm grasp before releasing the glass. "*Romanée Conti.*"

"I'm sorry...?"

"*Romanée Conti* is one of the finest *pinot noirs* in all of France."

"I don't know my French wines, sorry." I took a sip and allowed the flavor to coat my lower lip and tongue. Delicious.

He watched me, eyes fixated on my mouth.

"It's wonderful." I licked my lip, not allowing any to go un-savored.

"I'm glad you approve. My wife was the connoisseur." He fiddled with the ring on his left ring finger.

"Is she going to join us?"

He took a seat in the chair opposite me, sighed and crossed his legs. He looked deep into his glass of wine, running his finger around the rim. "No. I'm sorry. She passed away a few years ago."

"I am so sorry." Nice way to stick my foot in my mouth.

"Everything you see here, including who I am, is all her doing."

Now he really had my attention. I sat forward in the chair, dangling my wine over the arm.

"What happened?" Ever since I uncovered my father's treachery, my curiosity and suspicion often times compelled me to ask more questions than were socially appropriate. A pained look crossed his face. "If you don't mind me asking? I don't want to bring up old memories."

He exhaled a long breath and leaned back in his chair. "No, it's OK." He paused. "It was the cancer. I wasn't able to save her in time, but her death fueled my focus. I hunted the horrid disease until it could no longer hide."

"Again, I'm so sorry about…"

"Lydia."

"Yes…Lydia. I can't thank you enough for what you did for my sister and my family. Her death was not in vain." Guilt hit. I'd benefited from her death.

"That's what keeps me going." His face brightened for a moment. "I'm close to isolating another."

"Fantastic news. Is that why I'm here? Are you preparing to go to market?"

He looked down at his hands. "Not exactly. You are not here on business. I probably should have explained sooner."

Now that was news. I sat up straight. "I'm afraid I don't understand."

"I suspect not. It's not the kind of thing one can place in a letter. But the moment I saw you in Kansas City…"

Kansas City? Oh no. I had almost forgotten he'd said he had been there. That moment in time where everything I had worked for left to join my childhood. "Doctor, my behavior in Kansas City was inappropriate. My apologies, but I don't think I understand."

He smiled. "No need to apologize. After your speech, I had to get to know you. I need you."

I laughed and looked down, trying to hide my schoolgirl

blush. The great Dr. Vincent needed me? There were many ways I'd love for him to need me. Surely, I wasn't in Paris to walk his cat? I toyed with a button on my suit jacket and cleared my throat. "What can I do for you?"

"Do you know what my wife did for a living?"

"No. There isn't much written about you, or her from a personal perspective. I didn't even know she had passed."

He smiled. "Did your homework, did you, Ms. Watkins?"

The playful tone in his voice was welcome, given the heaviness of the conversation. "I tried, but you don't give up much."

"You're right. Before I started doing cancer research, I was a successful, practicing neuropsychiatrist. Understanding how behavior and brain function relate is the key to solving many debilitating psychiatric illnesses. But when working so closely with patients, keeping one's private life concealed is essential. Some patients can make unhealthy connections because, to understand why they do what they do, you must know their secrets."

"I can imagine. Was it a hard jump from private practice to research?"

"Yes. I miss the patient interaction. The way the human mind works fascinates me. Did you know people wear their ethics on their sleeves? Most don't look for it, but I can tell when someone is trustworthy."

If only I'd had that skill, lives might have been saved.

He took a sip of wine and the slightest bit dripped onto his chin. He lifted it with his finger, placed the droplet on his tongue and sucked his finger into his mouth. "You are trustworthy."

I pretended not to notice, but warmth ignited between my legs. The man was sex in a suit—sensual without even meaning to be. Knowing he wasn't married somehow opened a world of possibilities I'd never considered.

He leaned forward, directing his full attention at my rosy cheeks.

His words finally pulled me from my daydream. "Huh? Oh... Really?"

"Yes. Why do you think there is so little written about me? It isn't that people don't know my secrets. It's because I only impart them to those who would never betray me."

"You'll have to teach me that trick. It might have saved me a lot of heartache." I turned my focus to the crackling fire in the hearth.

He laughed. "Ah... Matters of the heart are tricky. I find it best to avoid them. But don't be hard on yourself. The closer you are to someone the less perceptive we become. Perhaps you'll leave here knowing a little more about yourself than you did when you got here."

I met his gaze. "I'm learning already."

"Good. Are you tired? It was a long flight." He reached down into the side of the chair and pulled out a folder previously obscured by the cushions and sat it on his lap.

"I am, but there's no way I can sleep until you tell me why I'm here?"

"Curious? Are you looking to open Pandora's box? You know, not every box is filled with disaster. Some contain the world's greatest treasures." He smiled.

Even though I knew the box could have come from no one other than him, his words were a subtle confirmation. "So it was you? The box, I mean."

He lifted the wine to his lips. "Yes." He sipped. "You needed a place to rest your demons. We all have them, but if we lock them away, we can keep them from draining our pleasures."

He set his glass on the table beside him, leaned forward and handed me the folder. "Speaking of pleasures… Please wait to open it until I tell you."

"OK." I reached out, took the folder and laid it in my lap.

"I met my wife when I was in med. school. She was my instructor specializing in sexuality—specifically, sexual dysfunction. She moved to America to study the role of inhibition in American culture."

"Sounds interesting, but if she was an instructor and you were a student…"

He took a deep breath. "Yes. You are beginning to see. When it came to sex my wife loved to blur lines and defy social norms." He cleared his throat. "I became a challenge. Abuse in early childhood lead to my adoption by a very loving and supportive family, but it left its mark. We married after my graduation." He stood, picked up his wine glass and walked to the fireplace. He stared into the flames and continued, "Our marriage was not…conventional. My wife's desire to push boundaries and my hang-ups from childhood lead to a unique arrangement."

This was not the conversation I expected. "Doctor, you don't need to tell me all of this. It's personal…"

"Ah, but it's essential." He took a sip of wine.

Where in the hell was this going? I shifted in my seat.

"It took years of coaching until I was comfortable orgasming in front of another human being."

The gulp of wine I'd taken to speed through the conversation caught in my throat. I began to cough. Whoa. When the good doctor decided to share, he really shared. Why on earth did I need to know this?

"Are you all right, Elaine?"

One last sputter. "Yes. Sorry. Go on." I smiled, hoping to mask my distress.

"Lydia was fascinated by me, but our relationship took a turn when we fell in love. Unfortunately, we never made love in the conventional sense. We compromised. It was her understanding and love for me that helped us. She had sex with others while I watched and directed. Her needs for physical connection were fulfilled and by calling the shots, I was able to be a participant. It gave me a sense of control, and eventually, I learned enough to let go somewhat."

I grasped the folder in my lap tighter and sat up. Why was he telling me this? "I'm so sorry," was all I could think to say.

"Nothing to be sorry about, we had a wonderful, fulfilling marriage. When one engages in the abnormal long enough, it becomes normal. I loved her with all my heart and have no doubt she loved me. It was our intimacy."

I crossed my legs and placed the folder beside me, hoping to fake comfort during the strange conversation. "It's good that you found each other, sounds like she was an amazing woman."

He returned to the chair, placed the glass on the side table and sat. "It's been a long time since her death, and even longer since I've known companionship. I won't give up my job for a relationship. How could I explain all of this?"

I tried to address him with the same clinical tone he used. "You don't seem to have a problem telling me."

"Only because I've been rehearsing this conversation in my head for two years. Remember the presentation you gave at the convention in Kansas City?"

I shifted and re-crossed my legs and gripped the arms of the chair. I hid my confusion over his change of subject, and answered with a simple, "Yes."

"I knew then, if I was to try this crazy idea, it had to be with you. I told myself in Kansas City, if our paths ever crossed again, it would be my sign. Speaking with you in the meeting last week, steeled my resolve."

"You don't seem one to bank on fate. Wait… What crazy idea? I'm still not quite sure what you are asking."

"Open the folder." He gestured toward it.

I opened the cover. A photo of the most beautiful nude man filled the page. He was perfection. The side angle of the photo hid nothing—his firm muscles in his tight, rounded ass, and his massive erect cock were exposed to my eyes. His dark hair hung in waves to his shoulders, featuring the sharp angle of his jaw and straight nose. My mouth ran dry.

"That's Marco. Exquisite isn't he? He's as smart as he is handsome and he is a dear friend." He laced his fingers together and leaned forward to gaze upon the picture. "Turn the page. Sebastian."

The man on the next page matched the first man's beauty. His short, cropped blond hair framed defined Scandinavian features, and his tall build was toned and unblemished.

"Doctor, what are you asking?"

"I'm asking you to surrender to five days of passion. To discover physical delights you've never known and will never know again."

I stared at the doctor, at the photos, then back again.

He pointed to the page. "I want to watch those two men ravish you under my direction."

It had to be a joke or one of those "gotcha" reality TV shows. He couldn't possibly be serious. "I'm not a prostitute!" I stood, readying to leave.

"Of course you're not." He stood and grabbed my hand. "I didn't mean to imply that you are. You'll notice I've made you no promises. There isn't a promotion or prize for doing this. I'm simply hoping you'll choose to indulge me. There is something about you, Elaine. I would work to seduce you, if I was capable of it, but this is what I have to offer."

I pulled my hand out of his. "This is crazy! You want me to sleep with these men so you can get off watching."

"No. I want to tell these men how to touch your body so that I can bring you pleasure. It will be me making love to you. I chose them to make the experience as stimulating as possible. Understand, in all of this, it's me who is in charge; it's me you'll be intimate with. Those two men will be an extra set of lips, an additional tongue, another cock at my disposal to make you writhe."

His words did things to me—a strange, hot seduction.

"Why two men?"

"Ever made love to two men at once?"

I wasn't a prude by any means but… "No!"

"It was Lydia's favorite indulgence on special occasions. And you, my dear, are special." He grasped my upper arms and fixed me with his gaze. "I want our time together to be memorable. Perhaps I'm selfish for wanting to give you an experience you'll never be able to duplicate. But isn't that every man's desire when he makes love to his woman?" He squeezed my arms tighter and pulled me closer to him.

I couldn't breathe. It was all so unbelievable. Heat was building between my thighs and I tried to look away from him, but couldn't.

He released my arms. "After this week you return home and nothing changes."

"Just like that. Nothing changes?"

I turned, picked up the folder, and slumped into the chair. I opened the folder, looked at the photos again and then back to the doctor. "And if I don't agree?" Would I be fired?

He sat and crossed his legs. "You can go sightseeing for a

week or whatever you choose." He leaned forward. "Paris is a lovely city, but you'll always wonder what it would have been like. Imagine just how good it might have been." He leaned back again. "Either way, you choose. When you return home, you go back to being you and I remain me, half a world away. Prostitution is a financial transaction; I have no interest in that. What I'm asking is for you to be my lover for this one week in Paris."

I put my face in my hands. This was a train wreck. What in the hell was I going to do?

"If you choose to indulge me, you'll discover ecstasy that few ever experience. I don't want your answer tonight. You're tired and in need of a good night's sleep." He stood and reached for my hand. "Let me show you to your room."

Speechless. I stood, but took the glass of wine instead of his hand. I would need it. Stowing the folder under my arm, I followed him out of the room and up the winding staircase.

At the door to my room, he paused. "Elaine, there is no pressure. I only want this to happen if you want it to. If you have any doubt, please decline. I have no desire to force your will. I chose you of all the women I see day in and day out for several reasons—your confidence, for one. It tells me you'll see the offer for what it is—an opportunity. Your strong independence will let you see this situation without gender bias. Someone weaker would allow social norms of what a woman should do, or not do, sexually get in the way of enjoyment. You will not and that is important to me."

"You don't know me. This is insane." I brought the glass to my lips and drained every last drop.

"Is it? It was your compassion that sealed the deal for me. You can see past my limitations, just as you did your father's, and your honesty and ethics will keep you from destroying me with this knowledge if you choose to walk away. Is that insane?"

"Yes. Yes it is." I reached for the door handle.

"Sleep on it. Look over the files. Remember, you are in a foreign city. No one will ever know." He leaned in and kissed me on the cheek, but paused to breathe in my ear, "I would be ever so grateful." He allowed his words to settle in before saying, "Sweet dreams, my Elaine."

I turned the handle and stumbled through the door. The photos of the nude men, along with various other pieces of paper, scattered across the floor. I bent over to pick them up, hand still on the knob. I paused and stared at the man labeled Marco, with the over-sized penis. Damn! Did they really make men like that? The feeling of being watched overcame me and I lifted my eyes to find the doctor observing with a mischievous grin.

"Good night, Doctor." I slammed the door.

\* \* \*

Insanity. He couldn't be serious, could he? I stared at the photos again and leafed through the paperwork while peripherally taking in the beauty of the old-world French decor. The room was lovely, with its black and white patterns and plush linens, but I couldn't stop looking at the pictures. Who agrees to something like this? My first reaction to most things was to apply logic. Find the easiest path, the quickest, safest solution. Was he right? If I were to say no, would I be consumed with "what if?" later on? Would not knowing what could've happened be a bigger burden than the memory of the wildest sex romp of all time? I was in Paris on his whim for Christ's sake. Could I go through with it? Could I not?

"Damn you, Dr. Vincent." It was just sex after all. I'd had my share of experiences and appreciated the need to scratch an itch, but never did I think to involve an audience. The men he'd chosen were beyond gorgeous, but it was the doctor's charm and intellect that I found most appealing. If he had simply asked me to be his lover, we would have been naked in front of the fire before the night was out, but this was new territory. These other men were strangers. Still, the one named Marco's come-hither stare was tantalizing. In high school I had fantasized about my two best friends dragging me behind the stage and having their way with me, so my curiosity was piqued.

What person in their right mind turns down Dr. Vincent? What person in their right mind agrees to his arrangement? Could I have sex with someone watching, especially if that someone was him?

I sighed, "Stan's kids. I'll consider it for Stan's kids." I said it out loud, but it was the weakest excuse of all. Still, temptation had me reaching for anything. I picked up the extra papers and placed them on the dresser. A hot shower, a good night's sleep and a prayer for clarity were in order.

## CHAPTER FOUR

# LE JULES VERNE

T HE NEXT DAY, THE PARIS SUNLIGHT STREAMED THROUGH the cracks in the black and white patterned drapes in Dr. Vincent's guest room. But it was the decorative garment bag sitting on the nightstand that caught my eye.

Attached to the front with a ribbon was a small envelope. I removed it, and then slid my finger along the seam. I pulled a card with a large 'V' on the front from the paper.

*Dearest Elaine,*

*I hope you have rested well and that your dreams were sweet. I pray my offer is a distraction big enough to eclipse all your troubles.*

*Please forgive me, I have a few errands to run this morning, but please make yourself at home. Pierre will take you wherever you would like to go, but I do hope that you'll consider joining Marco, Sebastian and me at Le Jules Verne tonight at 6:00 PM. I have picked out something special for you to wear, should you chose to join us.*

*With love,*
*Xavier*

*P.S. You are just as beautiful when you sleep.*

Distraction, indeed. Maybe he had a point.

* * *

The car door opened. Dr. Vincent's driver helped me out. I looked up at that great work of art—the Eiffel Tower. I didn't know it had a restaurant inside. The doctor's flair for the dramatic knew no bounds.

The dusty rose awning that covered the iron stairs read, Le Jules Verne. The crisp Parisian air filled my lungs causing a shiver to rush through my body. Was it a chill, or fear of the unknown?

"Thank you." I nodded to Pierre.

He returned the gesture, but otherwise remained still, with his hands clasped behind his back.

When I'd agreed to dinner, a small French bistro had come to mind, not this. What the hell was I thinking? Would I be able to refuse him? Did I even want to? As the doctor indicated on his card, I had been looking for a distraction from the hailstorm of my life. *Careful what you wish for.*

I took each step slowly, hiking the hem of the blue velvet dress I'd found in the bag earlier that morning. The metal of the great structure amplified the click of my heels.

After thinking all night and spending all day drinking in the Paris sunlight that saturated the veranda attached to my quarters, I had decided not knowing what could have been would be the greater burden. Was I crazy? Perhaps. Was I certain? Absolutely not. But I was decisive.

I was confident enough to make the choice and live with it, but what steeled my decision was a deep seated hope entwined with guilt; hope that I might give back more than a vicarious thrill to repay him for benefiting from his loss. The doctor had changed my life forever. Could I do the same for him?

This was it. No turning back.

I didn't pass a single person on the way to the elevator, which seemed odd, given the bustle of nightlife on the street outside.

The doors opened into a beautiful modern restaurant filled with empty tables. It was silent except for soft, vintage French music playing overhead. The windows that lined the space provided a breathtaking view of the city.

"Mademoiselle, if you'll follow me." A man in his twenties, wearing a black tie, white shirt, black pants and a white linen napkin tucked into the waist of his half-apron, lead me to a half-booth, a black leather bench on one side and two chairs on the other, that sat against the far wall. "Dr. Vincent and his associates will be here shortly." His English was perfect but accented. He motioned me toward the black leather bench-seat.

Mesmerized by the twinkling city lights, I stared out the window as the *maître d'* poured water into a glass on the table before taking his leave.

"Breathtaking." With just one word the doctor lit a flame— the promise of things to come.

"Yes, it is." I turned, confirming it was indeed him. In his black business suit and red tie, the doctor exuded sophistication. His American accent hinted at his highbrow schooling.

"Not Paris. You. When I imagined you wearing that dress

I didn't think there could be a more pleasing picture, but seeing you now... You are exquisite."

I folded my hands in my lap and focused on them, not wanting him to see the blush that flooded my cheeks, caused by the heat he triggered in me far too often. He pulled out his chair. As soon as he sat, the waiter filled his glass with sparkling water. The man paused and asked, "Your usual vintage, Doctor?"

"Yes. Thank you, Jacques."

"Where is everyone?" I couldn't imagine a tourist attraction being closed with the amount of foot traffic outside.

"This place is ours for the evening. We have...important matters to discuss." He winked. "I figured the fewer spectators the better."

I raised the glass to my lips and swallowed hard. "Yes, very wise."

A smile crossed his face. "I can't tell you how pleased I am that you came tonight. As nervous as I'm sure you have been, the uncertainty gnawed at me all night. I know it's a lot to ask."

"It is a lot to ask. I can't promise I'll be able to see it through."

"The fact that you are willing to try means more than you will ever know. A few housekeeping things..."

The waiter placed two glasses of red wine on the table and a tray of cheeses.

The doctor took the small knife and sliced off a thin piece, placed it on a cracker and handed it to me. He spoke as he prepared his own, "You saw the medical files I included with the photos. Marco and Sebastian have been tested. There is no risk to you, and for their safety, you were tested during your physical last week."

"What?" Son of a bitch! The crumbs of the cracker stuck in my throat. I coughed.

"I'm a medical doctor, Elaine. I called in a favor with Dr. Lawrence. I told her that you agreed to participate in one of my studies as a control subject and that I needed additional samples." He took a sip of wine.

"You had no right."

"You're right, but for this to work I had to make sure everyone was safe and needed to know you were taking precautions. The only lasting consequence I want from this encounter is for you to get wet every time you think of me."

Little did he know, he already had his wish, but it didn't trump the fact he'd overstepped his bounds. "Doctor, I don't think this is such a good—"

"Marco. Sebastian. Welcome." The doctor rose and motioned for the men to sit beside me, one on either side, flanking me on the bench-seat.

Holy shit. Men like that *did* exist. Their pictures didn't do them justice. And there was no mystery to what lurked behind Marco's zipper. Whoa. Deep breath.

"Marco. Sebastian. This is my Elaine."

Marco took my hand out of my lap and brought it to his full lips and kissed the back. "Elaine. It is all my pleasure." His dark hair made him look mysterious and ruggedly handsome.

"Elaine. This is Marco."

I stared at the man as his hand grasped mine. Blink, I needed to blink. "Ah...hello." The doctor was handsome—a young, Pierce Brosnan gorgeous. Marco was romance novel cover model perfect. Would I survive?

The doctor looked toward the other man in his dark business suit and tie. "Sebastian, isn't she lovely?"

Sebastian took my hand from Marco's and brought it to

his lips. "Lovely doesn't do her justice, X." His soft, warm lips touched my skin for a moment.

The doctor relaxed in his seat. "Elaine was just telling me that she was having second thoughts."

I looked for any trace of smugness on his face, but there was none to be found. Simple fact.

"Won't you at least enjoy a meal?" A heavy Italian accent amplified Marco's sex appeal. The waiter returned and placed a glass of wine in front of him. "No one will force you into anything. If you change your mind, it's fine."

"Fine, but I'm not happy you invaded my privacy." I glared at the doctor.

"I'm sorry. I hope that you understand, I meant you no harm. Marco is a close friend of mine—my protégé of sorts. He's one of the scientists on my team and I need to make sure he is safe if we ever want to see another cure. Sebastian is a fellow doctor, a close family friend. And you... You are my sole purpose for existing this week. Please understand."

"So, I'm the only stranger?"

"Yes. But I told you trust is important to me. They would never do anything to hurt you. We've all taken the oath to heal, not harm. Besides, it's not like the three of us have seen each other in this capacity. This is a new experience for all of us. So, if you're worried, you could say that we're all virgins in this play."

Sebastian laughed. "Yes, but you won't have the unfortunate experience of having images of Marco's hairy ass pop into your head, making for all kinds of awkward scenarios."

Marco reached around me and pointed to Sebastian, "I'll have you know, my ass is not hairy. I had it waxed last week."

The doctor shot them a condemning look and said, "I think Elaine gets the point."

"So, you're all doctors?" I looked from the doctor, to Marco and then Sebastian.

Marco chuckled. "Yes, but they like to tease me that I don't count since I've never directly treated patients outside of med. school. Give me a petri dish and a microscope any day."

This was crazier than I thought. I looked at Marco. "You're OK with this?"

"Xavier has been my friend for a very long time. I want to help him, and it's not as though we don't get something out of it. You're a beautiful woman. It would be my honor to give you pleasure for days on end. Has he told you what he likes best?" He glanced at the doctor.

Was that a blush on the good doctor's face? "No. He hasn't."

"He likes to watch a woman come. So it's our job to keep you on the edge of ecstasy for the next week. Of course, only if you agree." He took a sip of wine, gazing at me over the rim of the glass.

I didn't answer, but took a gulp of my own.

* * *

"And then Xavier said, 'Oh fuck it. I'm going to Barbados.' We all thought he was kidding. Several hours later, he sends us a picture of his pasty white feet with the ocean in the background. That's how he deals with stress." They all laughed.

"That's too funny." I chuckled and washed down a bite of chocolate soufflé with the heady wine. I wasn't sure if it was the wine, the food, or the fact that the men seemed so at ease with the situation and each other, but my nerves had settled and I enjoyed the company.

In the several hours that had passed, Marco painted a picture of Dr. Vincent as a man who loved the people he worked with and who garnered the same respect. Sebastian told embarrassing stories of drunken holiday parties and the doctor's fondness for art. The bond between the three men was undeniable and as the wine flowed, the tension in the room eased.

Dr. Vincent glanced out the window and sighed. "Elaine… my sweet, would you do me a huge favor?"

I wiped a smudge of chocolate from my lip with the napkin. "Sure. What do you need?" I popped the last morsel of the decadent dessert into my mouth.

He leaned across the table, locked his gaze with mine. "I want you to slide that velvet up your thighs until it's gathered at your waist. Then I want you to take your panties off and hand them to me. Can you do that for me?"

I stopped chewing and stared.

His steel blue eyes mesmerized. "Elaine, you are so beautiful. Please, I want to see you. All of you."

The choice was mine. But was there really one? A decision between 'what if' and 'remember when.'

Trapped in his sights and between his two beautiful friends, I chose to stop thinking. As if commanded, I gathered the hem of the dress in my fists and lifted. Lace tickled my legs as I pulled my panties free of the first foot, then the other. Still shielded by the tablecloth, I handed the small strip of fabric to the doctor.

He rolled them up and placed them in his pocket. He pulled the table toward him so I was no longer obscured. "Did you know there's a connection between the shape of a woman's mouth and her ability to orgasm?"

I swallowed hard. "Ah… no." His brilliant eyes reflected the specks of light cast by the city.

"You can see it. When I looked at you for the first time…" He reached out and outlined my lips without touching me. "It's right there. It tells all. When you're in a public place and desire hits, do you rub your thighs together? Do you look around and wonder if anyone knows your secret? Well, I do."

I couldn't speak. He was right. I had always been in touch with my sexual side. In the theater, in my classes, in meetings at work, I worked myself to the brink of orgasm with only my thoughts and clenching muscles. It was my guilty pleasure. My dirty little secret. Sometimes I failed to stop short. Damn, he was good.

"How many times do you indulge? Once is never enough, is it? Dozens. I bet you're swollen and ready and we haven't even started. Let me see."

I often explored my body, but always when I was alone. An audience was new territory. We were in a restaurant. Granted a nearly empty one, but… Opening my legs would be the tipping point. I could still change my mind.

Marco leaned in and whispered in my ear, "Show him." His hot breath tickled. I shivered. He placed his hand on my thigh, giving the slightest nudge. Sebastian placed his palm on my knee.

My leg twitched without my permission, but Marco took it as a sign of victory. I closed my eyes as his hands, smooth, large and masculine, urged them apart. The cold breeze from the air conditioning blew across my wet flesh, chilling. The thought of these three men eyeing me with lust boiled my blood.

A gasp left the doctor's lips. "Even better than I imagined."

I couldn't breathe. Was it embarrassment or anticipation? Or the heady combination of the two? What an intoxicating mixture.

"Marco, open her up to me. Show me all she hides."

Sebastian caressed my thigh, while Marco scraped his stubble along my neck and grasped my chin with one hand.

His lips captured mine, soft and full, tasting of wine and chocolate. His other hand ran up the inside of my other thigh and then he rested his fingers between my slick folds.

I moaned when Sebastian's lips found that sensitive spot behind my ear.

Marco halted his kiss and directed his attention back to the doctor. He parted my folds. "What do you think, Xavier?"

The doctor leaned across the table. "She's perfection."

Just then Jacques appeared with another round of water. I tried to close my legs but Marco and Sebastian held them open with a firm hand on each thigh.

Dr. Vincent motioned for Jacques. "Jacques, tell me. Is that not the most beautiful pussy you've ever seen?"

"Yes, it is Doctor. By far."

"What do you think I should do? She's dripping wet."

Jacques folded the towel that was once wrapped around the bottle of sparkling water and tucked it under his arm, then placed the glass on the table. "She's begging to be fucked. I say do what any gentleman would, and give the lady all she desires."

The doctor nodded. "Good answer. You always give the best advice."

Jacques turned and walked toward the kitchen like this was an everyday occurrence. I had heard that the French were more blasé about sex, but the waiter's comfort with the situation made me wonder what else he may have witnessed in his role.

Dr. Vincent leaned back in the chair and fumbled with his pants. The thought of him touching himself because of me added a new emotion to the mix. Then he spoke, "You heard the man, Marco. Fuck her… With your fingers."

I couldn't have uttered a sound if I had wanted to. The scene was too surreal.

Marco slid his fingers through my wetness and entered me with one long digit. Marco's cock pressed hard against my leg. He slid his finger in and out. Every time he pushed his finger back inside, he rubbed his cock against me.

The doctor unzipped the fly on his pants. "Sebastian, show me her breasts."

Sebastian slid the sleeves of the dress down my arms. He reached behind me, urging me to lean forward and unhooked my bra. He bunched the dress at my waist and removed the remaining confining garment. I had never been a thin woman and always considered my breasts one of my finer features. My nipples stood hard, accenting the full, round globes.

Sebastian's hand rose as if to touch them, but the doctor interrupted, "Not yet, I want her to think about you touching them first. Let it sink in. The brain is the most powerful sex organ. I want her to think about you touching and sucking them. Marco, add another finger, she needs more."

"My pleasure." Marco's fingers were long and he curved them so each time he breached my core they hit a place that sent electricity through my body.

Marco moaned against my neck. "You're like silk. So tight. I can't wait to fuck you." His fingers moved faster and his palm grazed my clit with each penetration.

I opened my eyes to see the doctor leaning back in the chair, his pants unzipped and his cock in his hand. The size of him surprised me. What a waste that no woman would ever know the pleasure of having him. He caressed it with long, confident strokes; his eyes darted from mine to Marco's work and back.

The doctor released a sound somewhere between a moan

and hum. "Marco, fuck her harder, I want to see her come."

Marco complied. His hand moved in frantic motions, pulling all the way out then slamming back in rapid succession.

"That's it Marco. Work her juicy pussy." Sucking sounds filled the air. "Sebastian, she's ready. Do it now."

Sebastian's large hands grasped my breast and his mouth closed over my nipple. He sucked hard, and teased with the tip of his tongue.

I moaned, tossing my head back. I was close but still fraught with anxiety.

The doctor leaned to the side. "Look in the glass."

In the window, the superimposed image of Marco's performance, Sebastian latched on to my breast and the doctor's hand wrapped around his own cock, reflected back at me.

I tried to hold back, but it was too much. I came undone. My legs went rigid and my muscles closed around Marco's fingers. I groaned, trying to choke back a scream. A cloud of euphoria filled my head and in that moment I didn't care where I was or why I was there. It was peace. A warm gush of liquid coated my thighs, Marco's hand, and the bench. I threw my head back and gritted my teeth while his fingers maintained their movement. I fought to remain in the moment, riding every last jolt of electricity.

Soon the gravity of reality took hold, and little by little brought me back. My breathing labored, Marco's rhythm slowed and Sebastian released his hold, while I recovered from the most intense experience of my life.

"Oh, Elaine. I could not have chosen better." Dr. Vincent beamed.

I struggled for words to respond, but they wouldn't come.

The doctor shifted in his seat. Still erect. Still free. "Marco, it seems you made a mess. Why don't you go ahead and clean that up?"

"Gladly." Marco smiled and dropped to his knees. When he pushed my legs open wider, draping one over Sebastian's lap, I felt the brush of stubble on the inside of my thigh.

"What are you... Ahhh..." With the first swipe of his tongue, I lost all desire to object.

Marco's tongue delved, flicked and fucked its way between my legs. I squirmed, but his hand held my hips in place.

"Marco. I. Oh." I couldn't speak.

The doctor's breathing was ragged. "How does she taste, Marco?"

Marco lifted his head from between my legs. "Like. Fucking. Heaven. I can't get enough." Face first he lunged again, his shadow-beard scraping the sensitive flesh, leaving a delicious burn. He pulled on my hip, forcing a snug fit against his face. His nose teased, while his tongue explored.

The doctor's strokes took on a frantic pace and my mind focused on one goal. "Elaine," He groaned. "Do you like watching me as much as I like watching you?" He smoothed his hand over the pre-cum that beaded at the top of his erection. "Do you see what you do to me?"

He was right. I did like watching him. There was nothing sexier than watching a man as powerful as him command his own cock. In that moment, I formulated a plan of my own. I wasn't the only one with demons that needed to be caged.

The doctor panted, "Sebastian, kiss her. Fuck her mouth with your tongue, while Marco fucks her pussy with his."

The doctor's crass instructions ignited a fire in me. Sebastian cupped my chin, turned my head toward him and swallowed my moan.

Marco nipped my clit with his teeth. My body jerked at

the sensation and forced Marco into the table, causing he tablecloth to slide and send a dessert dish crashing to the floor. Sebastian halted the kiss and the "yes" I intended to be seductive and confident erupted as squeal.

The doctor's shaft glided through his fingers as he pistoned his fist along his length.

Marco was not dissuaded by the incident and immediately focused the tip of his tongue on my clit. I didn't have much longer.

Dr. Vincent must have sensed it. "That's it. You're close. I can see it." His fist squeezed his erection tighter, his arm more rigid with each stroke. "Come on Marco's face. Drown him. I want to see your desire drip from his chin."

Those words and the tightening of Marco's fingers on my ass sent me crashing. I did as the doctor asked and let go. A growl-groan escaped my lips, while the rush that started between my legs flooded my brain. I fisted Marco's hair as wave after wave of pleasure consumed me.

Marco peppered my soaking flesh with soft kisses, and then lifted his head from between my legs. Just as the doctor ordered, drips fell from his chin leaving small, dark dots on his steel blue shirt. I turned to face Xavier who was biting his lip. Sweat highlighted his forehead and his cock stood hard, red and straining. He inhaled and breathed on the exhale, "Kiss her, Marco."

Marco crushed his lips to mine. The taste, a honeyed musk, invaded my mouth.

"Sebastian, it's time to get your fingers wet."

Sebastian cupped me between the legs. "She's so hot, wet and swollen, X." Starting with slow circles, he rubbed my clit, and then slid two fingers into me.

The doctor growled, "Fuck her harder."

Sebastian's fingers slid in and out, faster and faster, diving deeper with each thrust, while his thumb stroked my clit.

Marco moved back to give Sebastian room. He moaned, "Fuck. That's hot," while he watched Sebastian work my pussy.

The doctor's focus moved from between my legs to my face. We locked gazes. "Elaine, tell me what you want."

I couldn't answer.

"What do you want me to command him to do?"

Sebastian added a third finger and stretched, filling me.

I bit my lip to fight the wave of pleasure threatening to consume me.

"Elaine, tell me." The doctor's hand worked his cock to the same rhythm Sebastian's fingers fucked me.

More than my own orgasm I wanted his, but could I say it? I closed my eyes for a moment and when I opened them his intense, lust-filled stare gave me the courage I needed. "I want you to come. I want to watch you, Doctor."

"Fuck."

Marco turned to face the doctor.

Stream after stream of cum erupted from Dr. Vincent's cock, splattering his pants and shirt with his release.

I cried out, "Oh God," and gasped as euphoria claimed me once again, causing beads of sweat to collect at my throat. I came harder than I ever had before.

Sebastian captured my mouth with his and swallowed my moans. Once the quakes quieted, he kissed his way across my cheek, down my neck and chest, until he placed one final one on the swell of my breast.

The doctor's chest heaved from his heavy breaths. Slow, lazy strokes milked his shaft of every last drop.

Marco took his seat beside me, but kept his hand on my thigh.

We all sat in silence for a few minutes, savoring the moment.

With one of the black linen napkins from the table, the doctor cleaned himself and tucked his cock back into his pants before Jacques returned to wish us good night.

I looked at Marco, and then Sebastian. "What about you?" They were left unsatisfied.

Sebastian leaned in, kissed my cheek and said, "We're patient. Plenty of time left for us. Tonight is all about you."

Marco put his hand on my thigh and leaned forward to look at Sebastian. "Speak for yourself. I'm not patient. I'd fuck her right here on this table, if she wasn't having second thoughts just an hour ago." He leaned back and looked at me. "It's important for you to ease into this arrangement. You need to know you can trust us before we take this to the next level." He rested his back against the black, tufted leather seat back.

Sebastian's hot breath tickled my ear as he whispered, "Besides, we know what X has planned for tomorrow. We're going to need our strength."

The promise of things to come and his hot breath against my skin made me shiver. I pulled down my dress and both men helped me reequip my bra, but I wondered if the night's festivities were over, trying not to let the small amount of disappointment I felt show. I had assumed fucking them was part of the plan and if Marco's skills at oral translated to other things, I was in for a treat.

Dr. Vincent sat watching me with a grin of satisfaction. "I see you've been cured of second thoughts." It was a statement, not a question.

## CHAPTER FIVE

# MIRIAM

**H**AD I REALLY ALLOWED THAT TO HAPPEN? IN A RESTAU-rant, no less? Even though I was exhausted, slumber evaded me. By the time I managed to drift off, a smell permeated the air—bacon. Who could possibly be cooking at this hour? I pulled back the covers, reached for my phone on the nightstand. Nine AM? It felt as though my head had just hit the pillow, but jetlag be damned, the rumbling in my stomach was winning the fight. When my feet hit the floor, a yawn warred with my hunger on my unsteady walk to the *en suite* bathroom.

During my quick shower, I heard the door to the bedroom open, then close.

My curiosity could not be quenched. With the towel wrapped around my head like a turban and a soft, white, spa-quality robe obscuring my nudity, I cracked the door open for a peek.

On the bed lay a cream-colored, crinkled chiffon dress, with intricate embroidery embellishing the bodice—a short and whimsical style. I walked to the bed and opened the lid to the box sitting beside the dress. It contained sandals composed of bands of brown leather and beads. The small teal blue velvet pouch sitting on top of the shoes held a long string of pearls and a note.

*Dearest Elaine,*

*You are in for quite a treat today. I hope you don't mind that I took the liberty of selecting your attire again. You'll find I've provided everything you'll need for our little adventure. It's important to me that you are comfortable in the Paris heat.*

*When you are ready, please join in me in the kitchen. I have prepared breakfast for us.*

*Love,*
*X*

*P.S. You'll notice this ensemble is lacking undergarments; that is by design.*

Were those butterflies in my stomach? What was it about this man that made my skin tingle anytime he said or wrote my name? I should have been insulted that he'd tricked me into coming to Paris, even more so by his proposal, his invasion of my privacy, and his pushy wardrobe choices, but there was something about him—some kind of magnetism. Many might argue my gratitude for saving my sister, Gretchen, or perhaps his wealth fueled my fascination, but the desire ran far deeper.

The aroma of bacon grew stronger as I descended the stairs, dressed in the striking ensemble the doctor had chosen. Even though his insistence on dressing me remained a source of irritation, he did have excellent fashion sense.

The mansion, or perhaps castle was more accurate, was more stunning in daylight. The rich tones of the wool rugs, the raw silk drapes, the ironwork on the windows and stone everywhere, spoke of wealth centuries old. Even in my sandals each step echoed in the cavernous room.

In the kitchen stood a sight even more breathtaking than the house—the doctor. He stood in front of the large industrial stove, shirtless with a spatula in hand. His suits never betrayed his secret. As beautifully sculpted as Marco and Sebastian had been in their photos, the doctor was their rival.

He looked up from his task and stared. I averted my eyes, feeling guilty that I had been ogling him.

"Good morning, beautiful. You are exquisite. Somehow you manage to put to shame every one of my fantasies about you."

I dodged the compliment and swallowed the excitement bubbling through me. The idea the doctor fantasized about me pleased me more than it should have, but I had to gather my thoughts. "Isn't that dangerous?"

He smiled, "What's dangerous? Cooking? I love to cook. Between cooking and the gym, I almost forget how much I miss sex. That is until last night, I had almost forgotten how wonderful it is to connect with someone."

Or some ones. "I meant frying bacon without a shirt."

He scoffed. "I don't run from pain. I face it head on."

The irony in his statement was not lost on me. The pain of his childhood kept him a prisoner, yet he embraced physical pain. No one achieved a body like his without excruciating effort.

My contemplative moment was interrupted.

"You know what is painful? Trying to find American bacon

in Paris. I had to call in some favors. Come over and sit here beside me. Let me look at your loveliness." He pulled out a stool at the breakfast nook and patted it.

From the plate of crispy bacon he snapped the end off of a piece.

His outreaching hand surprised me. He held the morsel by the tips of his fingers just out of my reach. Was this allowed? I eyed his expression. Nothing out of the ordinary. It was a simple offering.

I leaned my head close and with my tongue coaxed the salty gift from his fingers, never touching him. As I closed my mouth Marco spoke, "You two starting without me?" He pulled a white T-shirt with black lettering over his smooth chest.

The doctor stood fixated on my mouth, while Marco walked to the breakfast nook and took a seat beside me.

"Good morning, Elaine." Marco placed a soft kiss on my lips. "Bacon. You shouldn't have, X."

"I didn't. Not for you at least. But since you'll be working up an appetite, it's probably best that you're well fed."

Marco laughed. "Yes, feed the beast."

I glanced at Marco and then to the doctor and back.

"I know you two are colleagues, but I don't get it. I could never imagine proposing this to anyone I work with."

The doctor placed more bacon on the plate. "Marco, and even Sebastian for that matter, are true friends." He then offered me another piece of the meat with the same careful gesture.

I took it, resisting the urge to lick his finger, and then laughed. "You do take BFF to a whole new level. I can honestly say I don't have anyone I could have enlisted if I were in your shoes."

It was the doctor's turn to chuckle. "It's not like I just floated the question out there. Both of them were relentless about trying to get me laid. I even dated someone, trying to fool them and everyone else for that matter, but no woman wants to deal with my hang-ups."

Marco reached over, grabbed the orange juice and poured some in a small glass. "If you hadn't picked a fucking psychopath to pretend with, you might have pulled it off. Man, you're a shitty shrink."

The doctor shot him a condemning stare, and pointed at him with the spatula. "That's it. No bacon for you." He turned back to me. "So, after I came clean over beers one night, the truth about my marriage came out. Marco immediately volunteered."

I looked at Marco. "It was really that easy for you?"

Marco sat forward. "Yes. I get to fuck a beautiful woman and help X at the same time; I didn't even have to think about it." He let out a little whine. "Ah, come on X, I take it back. You're not a shitty shrink. Give me some bacon."

X chuckled. "I'm letting you fuck my woman, I think that's enough. Get your own."

His woman? His statements of possession on some crazy level gave me comfort, and on another scared me to death. "What about Sebastian?"

They both looked at each other. Marco snickered. "You could say…he had a little encouragement." He jumped off the seat and made for the pile of bacon and scolded the doctor, "You're just jealous and getting old and cranky. You'll pay for that at your next workout."

"Marco doubles as my personal trainer. I figured it best; since I need his mind on my research, I'd better put his annoying habits to good use."

There was a friendly rapport between the two without a doubt. "How did the two of you meet?"

The doctor smiled. "When the university called and asked that I take an annoying know-it-all under my wing, I never imagined what I was getting into. He was at the top of his class and already had two revolutionary patents. The kid thought he ruled the world."

"Kid? I was twenty-one. Besides, you're only ten years older than me, or should I start calling you pops?"

The doctor shot him a scolding glance. "Anyway, I think I've said before I'm a pretty good judge of character and even though I wanted to drown him in the Rhine at times, I knew he was loyal and one of the most brilliant minds of our time. So I kept him. Now I don't think I could get rid of him."

"Was it the same with Sebastian?" I had to know.

"No. He's an esteemed physician here in France as well as a close family friend."

Marco spoke up, "I met Sebastian at the gym. I'm also his trainer."

"Wow, researcher, genius, personal trainer, is there anything you can't do?"

With his plate filled with bacon and a whole grain muffin, he stopped in front of me, bent down and placed a kiss on my cheek. "Sweetheart, you have yet to witness my finest talent." He winked.

I looked at the doctor. "And he's modest too."

"Nobody's perfect." Marco placed a plate in front of me along with a small glass of juice. He leaned in so close I could feel his breath on my ear. "Eat up. You're going to need your strength." He then took a seat beside me.

I swallowed hard, but the creaking of the front door interrupted my moment.

"Hello, Xavier. Xavier, Xavier, where are you?" A female voice with a thick French accent called.

The doctor folded his napkin and rose. "Excuse me. I have to greet our guest."

I glanced over at Marco. "Isn't Sebastian coming for breakfast?"

He chewed, swallowed, and then wiped his mouth with a napkin. "That's him, well his other half anyway."

"That can't be him. That's a woman's voice."

Marco started to choke on a laugh. "No. That's not him. Though it would be really funny if it was. That's Miriam."

"Miriam?"

He gulped. "His wife."

"Wife!" The word came out as a bellow. I quieted my voice to a forced whisper. "Oh my God. He's married. I can't believe... I didn't... Oh God... I've wrecked someone's marriage."

"Settle down. Has anything turned out like you expected since you got here?"

I paused. "No."

"Then what makes you think this is any different?"

Just then a squeaking caught my attention—like a bicycle tire on polished floors. In the doorway appeared the most elegant woman I'd ever seen, nestled in a wheel chair. The hum of the electric motor drowned out the shrill sound of the tire, as she grew closer. We made eye contact and the woman gasped.

"Oh Xavier, she's beautiful."

What was going on?

"I told Sebastian to trust you. Xavier, you have always had exquisite taste. That's one of the things that Lydia, God rest her soul, loved most about you." She pressed the steering stick and parked her chair just in front of me. She didn't look like she needed the chair, all of her limbs were intact, but the bag tied to her chair hinted at hidden problems.

"Let me get a look at you." She raised her hand slowly and it trembled as it would in a woman three times her age. Her smooth, creamy fingers wrapped around my hand as it continued to shake. "I can't thank you enough. You have my undying gratitude."

I wasn't sure what to say. What was I missing? "I'm sorry, but I…"

Dr. Vincent interrupted, "Forgive me, Miriam. Elaine only arrived two evenings ago. I didn't realize you would want to meet her, so I haven't exactly explained everything."

Her eyes grew wide. "Oh my…my dear…I can't imagine what you're thinking."

"I have to admit, I'm a bit confused." I shifted in my seat.

"Elaine. Even your name is lovely. I'm Sebastian's wife."

I tried to object, but she silenced me.

"This must seem so strange. Let me explain. Lydia and I were best friends since before we started grammar school. Our families were very close; I called Lydia sister. When she brought Xavier home to France, I couldn't have been more thrilled. When I met Sebastian at one of my shows, the puzzle was complete. Then tragedy struck, first with me and then with Lydia. I'm sure Xavier explained Lydia's passing. Right Xavier?" She shot him a scolding look.

"Yes. She knows."

"Well, several years before Lydia took ill, I developed an extremely rare and progressive form of MS. Most forms of Multiple Sclerosis are manageable with the new drugs on the market, but my condition is terminal."

I covered my mouth with my free hand to contain my gasp. "Oh, no. I'm so sorry."

"Oh, don't feel bad. There are worse ways to go. And I'm already cheating the fates. The textbooks said I should have died last year. Well, excuse my language, but fuck them. I'm not done yet."

I admired her spirit. I don't know that I could be so strong staring into the face of death. "I'm so sorry."

"Don't pity me, beautiful one. I've had it all—money, fame, fortune."

Marco set his fork on the plate. "Miriam was a prominent actress and sex symbol here in France. All Parisians know her face and her…"

"Marco! Yes, well it's hard to be a sex symbol with a colostomy bag dangling from your hip, but I still do appearances and fundraisers. I try to keep active."

"That's wonderful." I couldn't help but smile while her shaking fingers grasped mine.

"Now darling, the part that Xavier forgot to mention. After years of me harassing him to move on, and Lydia would have wanted it that way, he finally confessed to what he had planned for you. I know about his…ahhh…limitations and Lydia's love of men."

I cleared my throat. It was all so unbelievable.

She continued, "The one thing I love more than my next breath is my husband. He works day and night saving lives. He cares for me and I couldn't ask for anyone better. But in my condition, I can't give him what he deserves. As you can tell, I barely have the strength to squeeze your hand, and my legs no longer hold me. I've lost sensation over most of my body and the tubes make it impossible to feel sexy. He tries to help me but…I'm not stupid, Elaine. He's a beautiful man in the prime of his life and I'm fighting to hold on, but I don't know how much will be left of me in the end. There isn't much left now. He has never been selfish with me; I wanted to return the favor."

Xavier moved beside me. "I told her all about you."

She released my hand. "He did and it's perfect. I never wanted Sebastian to find comfort with a prostitute for obvious reasons, and I couldn't stand it if he fell in love. But a week of carnal indulgence is what he needs. Every man does. Elaine, I'm asking you to sleep with my husband. Allow him to indulge in the pleasures Xavier and Marco have planned for you. He's exceptionally talented. He told me you got a taste last night."

I wasn't sure if I could close my mouth. Marco was right; nothing ever went as planned here. I turned to my side to gauge his reaction and he winked and mouthed, "Told you."

"Miriam, while I…"

"Just say you'll do it. Unlike Xavier, I can't stay and watch. I need to have my memories of us. Please, make sure he enjoys himself. You won't be disappointed."

I hung my head in disbelief. Speechless. I really had to wonder if I wasn't in a coma somewhere, and this wasn't some weird manifestation of all of the naughty novels I had read.

She patted my leg. "Perfect. Xavier, can you help me to the door? My driver can take it from there."

"You're welcome to stay for breakfast." He moved one of the chairs in her path so she could turn the chair around.

"No, thank you. I have a few errands to run. Sebastian said he'd meet you at the gallery. What a magnificent place to start."

As he followed her out of the room, he responded, "I thought so. Should help set the mood."

I turned to Marco. "The gallery?"

"Yes, Lydia owned a gallery of erotic art and artifacts. Xavier thinks there are several pieces you'll appreciate." He picked up a slice of bacon from my plate and handed it to me. "Eat."

I bit off a piece and chewed. "You know this is all fucked up."

He laughed. "Yes, it is. Aren't we lucky?"

"I was thinking more like crazy."

## CHAPTER SIX

# COLLECTOR

After breakfast, I gathered my things for the day's festivities and headed to the car. The driver opened the door and helped me into the limo. Moments later, the doctor and Marco slid in on either side of me. Dr. Vincent pressed a button and a shaded panel slid into place obscuring us from the driver.

The engine hummed and the door closed, but it was the doctor's breath on my neck that held my attention.

"You smell so delightful. Like honey and sunlight."

I took a deep breath and reminded myself: this was all about sex. Nothing more. "Thank you."

He shifted in his seat and faced me. "You should be thankful for my hang up."

I turned toward him, wrinkled my brow and stared into his sapphire blue eyes. "Why is that? It doesn't seem to make you happy."

He leaned in closer, almost as though he would kiss me. "Why would you care about my happiness?"

Two could play his game. The attraction between us was dangerous and his close proximity only fueled the foreplay. I turned toward him, spreading my legs slightly and moved in closer, never releasing his gaze.

"But what if I want to see you happy?"

He laughed. "That's nonsense."

Marco remained quiet while I rebuked the doctor. "I'm insulted."

"Whatever for? We hardly know each other. Lust is one thing. It's superficial, honest and brief. Happiness, joy, love—those, my dear, are bonds that can't be broken and last an eternity."

"Who said anything about love? I just want to see you happy." I glanced out the window.

He placed a finger under my chin and forced me to look at him again. "So naïve. So foolish. That's the very definition of love. It's not hearts and flowers. It's caring about someone else's experience more than you care about your own." A wicked smile spread across his face. "Elaine, are you making a declaration?"

Normally, I would have challenged him, but embarrassment flooded my cheeks. I might have been younger than him, but I was far from a child. His condescending tone and too-close-for-comfort comment was overshadowed by his hand clutching the back of the seat in a vice-like grip with our mouths only inches apart. In that moment, when I stared into his soul, I made my vow. I would break his resolve and teach him that his games had consequences. He was not the only one capable of seduction. I neither confirmed nor denied his ridiculous claim.

"Oh dear Elaine, you do intrigue me, but you know what would delight me right now?"

"No, Doctor, what do you want?" Would he do it? Could this be it? Surely, it could not be that easy.

"You can tell me how much you want me," he whispered.

Stan was right: there wasn't anything small about Dr. Vincent, including his ego.

I laughed, while maintaining our standoff, and enunciated the word, "Never."

A grin, laced with mischief, pulled at the corners of the doctor's mouth. "Fine. Have it your way. Marco, lift her dress and tell me how much she wants me."

Marco complied, exposing me to his gaze. He placed a palm on my heat. "She's dripping, X. I think she likes you."

I did want him, but he was out of control. I let out a breathy sigh, which I prayed caressed his just out of reach lips, as Marco ran his fingers through my wetness.

"What if I don't want you?"

Marco slid a finger between my folds and slipped inside me. I gasped.

The doctor's gaze was intense. His dilated pupils, flushed cheeks and halting breaths betrayed him. "But you do. Remember, you can't lie to me. It might be Marco inside you, but never forget to whom you are making love. Marco, show her." He reached down and stroked his cock through the fabric of his black dress pants.

Marco inserted another finger and set a rhythm that was certain to undo me.

I gasped. Marco reached up and fisted his other hand in my hair, yanking my head back, exposing my throat. The jostling of the car drove him deeper inside as I felt the doctor's hot breath caress my ear. "He's fucking you with my permission. This week you are mine. No matter how good he feels, it's my face you'll remember."

I bit my lip. Marco drove me hard. Slamming his hand against my clit with each stroke. With each slap a grunt escaped. "What do you want from me?"

"Your passion." He licked his lips. "And anything else you are willing to give me."

Marco removed his fingers and replaced them with his mouth. His tongue slid between my folds on its journey to my clit.

I bit my lip and "Fuck," escaped on a breath. It felt so good.

The doctor moaned, while gripping himself through his pants. "God, that is so fucking sexy." He adjusted himself. "Come for me."

Marco's fingers rejoined the action. Son of a bitch, he was good.

One more thrust and the doctor's wish was fulfilled. My back arched further and I gripped the seat. Marco tightened his grip on my hair and a squeal tore through me, while my body clenched down on Marco's hand.

Marco mumbled, "So fucking tight," as he forced entry through my ecstasy, urging me deeper into bliss, only to stall with soft caresses from the inside out.

"I…ah… I'm…I…I'm" The flood of pleasure over came me and I closed my eyes, savoring the feel of Marco's work.

The doctor finished for me, "Beautiful. That's what you are."

Through my deep breaths and lust-filled head the words escaped, "If beauty doesn't make me worthy of *your* touch, Doctor, what will?"

He didn't pause. "It's not about worth. You are priceless. Like a piece of art or gem behind museum glass. Admired by all. Exquisite. Treasured. Collected."

Such pretty, dangerous words.

Marco removed his hand and lowered my dress.

I took the seat beside him. Patting Marco's leg in appreciation, I uttered one word. I couldn't let him do this to me. Allowing Dr. Vincent to become anything other than an interesting fuck would destroy me. I had to put a stop to it. "Borrowed."

"Come again?" The doctor shifted toward me.

Marco snickered. "Give her a minute. One at a time, X."

The doctor leaned back slightly and shot Marco the most disapproving look. "What did you say, Elaine?"

"I said, borrowed. You said collected. Treasured. I corrected you. A true collector does not discard a precious gem, never to think of it again. A collector preens over his works. Sets it upon a pedestal. Revels in the well-fought hunt. It's the possession that fuels his dedication. You, dear Doctor, are not a collector, you are a library cardholder and I am the story of the week."

Marco laughed and squeezed my thigh. "I like you more every minute."

Xavier Vincent stared out the window. Silence was his only response.

## CHAPTER SEVEN

# RAINMAKER

T HE CAR PULLED UP TO THE CURB OF A QUAINT FRENCH boutique. The cold shoulder I'd received for the remainder of the ride, made me ponder the possible changes in the doctor's plans. Was he so aggravated with me he'd send me on my way? The car door opened and his outstretched hand surprised me. I didn't know which lines could be blurred. Sometimes touching seemed allowed, but only when it was a formality. Perhaps he wasn't angry with me after all. The cobblestone street led to slate tiled sidewalks and to the window of *Désir Secrets*.

Beyond my reflection, photos of men and women in various seductive poses were accessorized with fresh flower accents to help soften the hard lines of each sculpted body. The floral arrangements and feminine architecture added old-world ambiance even while the art appeared minimal and modern.

Xavier steadied me by my elbow as I rose from the car. "This was Lydia's hobby," he said while pulling me to my feet.

I smoothed my dress but said nothing.

The doctor whispered something to the driver and Marco placed a hand on the small of my back.

The tinkling bells, hanging from the interior door handle, painted a mental picture very different from what greeted me. The room was expansive, stark white, and held no hint of the character the exterior ironwork and stucco hinted at.

It was a gallery—stripped down so the art became the focus.

From a side room emerged a beautiful, leggy woman. "Xavier," the woman said, breathy and seductive. He released my hand and approached her.

"Patrice! It has been too long." He took the woman's hand and kissed the back of it. Her large breasts overflowed the cups of her curve-hugging dress. She had a body any woman would die for.

"I thought we were beyond formalities." She kissed him on one cheek, and then the other and he returned the favor.

Xavier slid his arm around the woman's waist and something in me snarled. My body tensed. He wasn't mine. Damn him for all the extra words of adoration. Only sex. It's supposed to be only sex.

Marco noticed. "You don't like seeing him with her. Do you?"

"Why would I care?"

"Don't let my tight ass and good hair fool you; I'm not an idiot."

I glared at him for a moment, but couldn't keep my eyes off the doctor and the bombshell. "You're wrong."

"Elaine, I see it in your eyes every time you look at him. I don't know if you've fallen in love with him or the idea of him, but either way…"

"It's nonsense." I took a step away from Marco. And without thinking the words left my mouth, "Why is it so easy for him to touch her?"

"He's not having sex with her."

"Yet." I huffed.

"She means nothing to him. That's why it's easy."

I heard his words, but the way the doctor's hands slid up and down the woman's arms made me wonder. Watching his long fingers rest on her hip filled me with rage.

"I don't get it. He'd never touch me like that."

Marco stepped closer and wrapped his arm around me, pulling me closer. He breathed into my ear, "Exactly."

I ignored him.

The bells on the door chimed. Sebastian stepped through the door dressed in jeans and a leather jacket. He walked up beside me and whispered to both of us, "Sorry, I'm late."

Marco leaned in front of me making eye contact with Sebastian. "Hey, no problem. You're just to in time to witness the cat fight."

Sebastian laughed.

Marco put his arm around me, again. "Elaine here is going to kick Patrice's ass."

I removed his arm and stared at him. "What? I am not." I said it just a little too loud, because the doctor and Patrice glanced in our direction.

Sebastian chuckled.

The woman laughed, placed a soft kiss on his lips, grabbed her handbag and headed to the door. The kiss boiled my blood. Xavier followed her to the door and locked it behind her.

"Now where were we?" He stopped and stared at me. "Beautiful, what's wrong?"

"Nothing."

Marco laughed. "I don't think she likes Patrice."

The doctor turned to Sebastian. "Glad you could make it."

Sebastian responded, "Wouldn't miss it."

Xavier cleared his throat and took my arm, guiding me to a painting of a man and a woman in bed. The woman's legs were spread wide and the man rose above her. His cock was positioned to penetrate her.

"These works are some of the most precious pieces of erotic art you will ever see. Unlike me…my lovely Lydia was a splendid collector."

I glared at him. Obviously, he wasn't over the comment I'd made in the limo.

Still leading the way, he stopped in front of a painting of a woman being ravished by a horde of men. "Lydia studied several tribes in the Himalayas. There is limited inhabitable land, so this is how they control the population."

I snorted. "I'm sorry, but I would think an orgy would have the opposite effect."

He laughed. "You're right, if there was more than one woman involved. In their culture one woman takes many husbands. Often times a bride is selected for a family of brothers."

"That looks complicated. Couldn't she do them one at a time?"

"I'm sure she did, but this is her wedding night. Their job is to give her pleasure as one marital unit."

The dark skinned woman with the look of ecstasy in her eyes had a cock in every hole and a line of men prepped and ready. I stared in fascination, admiring the careful logistics needed to perform such an act.

Marco moved in behind me. "Have you ever had two men at once?"

"No." I crossed my arms.

He placed his hands on my hips. "Do you ever think about it?"

I shifted my weight to the other foot. "Not other than a passing fantasy from high school. I've never actually considered making it a reality."

"Think about it, Elaine. Think about men wanting you so badly, they can't wait." He reached under my skirt. "Think about having a cock in here." He slid his finger into me. "And one in here." He slid his finger between my cheeks and touched my rear entrance. I jerked.

Marco grabbed my hip. "Wait…has no one ever taken your ass?"

I didn't want to answer.

Xavier's intense stare was penetrating. "Elaine…" He took my hand in his.

"No. Never really considered it an option."

Xavier stroked my palm with his thumb. "We have so much to teach you."

In the center of the room stood an alabaster sculpture of a goddess—her nude body, draped in only beads while being caressed by two equally nude men. The men kneeled on either side of her, each with one of their hands between her legs. The woman's hands stretched to the heavens and in one she held a small box. Her unsurpassed beauty tarnished by the look of agony on her face.

The doctor moved to the front of the piece. "This is Pandora—a prominent figure in erotic art and literature. Throughout history there are many renditions of her story, but this particular artist had an interesting interpretation." He took a step to his left, admiring the work. "He did not believe that she released all evil in the world, but rather made a sacrifice. At the bottom of the box, beyond all of the agony she brought upon herself was a gift—a symbol that all hope is meaningless if one hasn't suffered. She raises the cleansed box to the heavens as her gift to the world while man grasps at hope."

The doctor proved to be quite the art aficionado. But the pressing question slid from the tip of my tongue, "The box you sent me, what did it mean?"

He turned to face me. "It always occurred to me that if she achieved her goal and released hope to the world, that real gift was that the box would be empty, and one by one we could fill it with the turmoil it once contained." He walked to me and took my hand. "I stood right here, the night the break-through came to me. You might give me credit for creating the drug, but I give credit to Pandora." He looked away as he spoke, but still held my hand. "When I saw your troubles that night at dinner, I wanted to take them away. All I kept thinking about was how much I hoped you'd agree to come to Paris. It was then I knew the box was empty and your suffering made you capable of seeing our rendezvous as an opportunity. I called in a few favors and had the box commissioned for you."

I squeezed his hand to get his attention. "That was very kind of you, Doctor, but we can't forget the dangers of hope. Hope unfulfilled is nothing more than sorrow." With Dr. Vincent I risked what I wasn't even willing to admit to myself—namely thinking that this week was anything more than sex. After a story like that, hope would surely destroy me.

His eyes grew wide. "You're probably right." He released my hand.

Marco placed his hand on my shoulder. I turned to him and he smiled, confirming he too understood the implications.

Sebastian followed at my side.

Next was the statue of a man bound and kneeling while staring at the ceiling. His huge, erect cock pointed heavenward. A stunning vision, but it was a large, gold-framed oil painting with vibrant red hues that caught my attention. I stared at an angel in a cage. Even though the door stood open, allowing his escape, his wings were clipped. His perfect nude body appeared weary from the tortures of a woman holding a whip.

The doctor whispered, "That is one of my favorites."

"It's powerful."

"It was a gift for my birthday from Lydia. She had it commissioned by one of the greatest erotic painters of our time."

"Sure beats a gift card."

He laughed. "Come on."

Genitals and entwined limbs were everywhere you looked. Marco slid his hand across my ass, gathered the fabric of my skirt in his fingers. The cold air brushed the skin of my cheek. He leaned down and whispered in my ear, "As if I wasn't pent up before all this sex…"

Xavier paused. "Sex has always been viewed as mysterious, powerful. Aside from the magic of conception, many cultures use it to bend the will of fate and gods alike."

The expansive room we entered next hung thick with shadows. Twinkling lights made to resemble a night sky sparkled and a large, artificial moon cast light on the two objects situated in the center of the room.

"Lydia's favorite story is that of the Rainmaker. It has become one of mine too."

"What is this room?"

"Ahhhh… One you are going to get to know very well, and I'm certain you will never forget." He walked to the center of the room toward a strange, wooden apparatus and a large throne. There were tables on either side of the wooden structure. Deep, midnight blue velvet curtains lined the walls.

"Through her research, Lydia uncovered a ritual used by a band of ancient Celts. Centuries ago, the king of the clan chose his queen and with only him did she lay until the dry season. It was believed the gods withheld the rain to demand offerings."

He took hold of my hand and led me to the wooden object shaped like a raised sawhorse but with smooth, rounded angles and odd indentations.

"On the first full moon, after the start of the dry spell, the king presented his queen as a tribute to the gods."

He must have noticed my wide eyes, because he chuckled.

"No love, not as a sacrifice. The king loved his queen. Women held much power. Though not a true matriarchal society, women were revered as givers of life—an extension of the Earth's powers. They believed a woman's body held the secrets to cure all." He smoothed his hand over the wooden beam.

"At twilight, the villagers gathered round and the king unveiled his queen, dressed in her royal robes."

The doctor's narrative skills, though outstanding, competed with another scene in the room.

Marco and Sebastian stepped out of their shoes and placed them under the table. They unbuttoned their pants, slid their zippers down and pushed them over their firm, sculpted asses, like synchronized swimmers. They undressed, folded their clothes and placed them on the table beside a black leather box. They were a magnificent sight to feast on.

Xavier continued to run his hands along the smooth wood. "The king said a prayer for rain and for his wife. And when the moon reached the proper position in the sky, he bound her to the Rainmaker."

Marco handed Dr. Vincent several black silk strands of fabric.

The doctor slid them through his fingers as he spoke. "Elaine, will you trust me?"

I crossed my arms. "I don't like pain."

He laughed. "Oh love, you need not worry about that. Please, trust me."

I paused. It was one thing to have sex with them, but while tied up? The control freak in me screamed, but the primal part of me that thirsted for adventure fueled the ringing in my ears.

"Please, Elaine. I assure you. You will not be disappointed."

I stared into his eyes, looking for any trace, even a remote spark, of a man like I saw in my father after I discovered his lies. Nothing. He hadn't lied to me yet. And after all I came here knowing I would have sex with Marco and Sebastian.

"Fine. But I don't want to be gagged."

"No worries, I want to hear you scream your passion."

Marco urged me to press against the Rainmaker by cupping my ass and pushing me forward. An indentation in the wood cradled my hips perfectly.

Sebastian pressed on my back urging me to bend to the contour of the apparatus. I remained standing, legs spread and bent at the waist to rest my chest on a long beam.

The doctor leaned down to whisper in my ear. "It's believed that if you apply the right pressure to the front of a woman's pelvis during sex, you can enhance her orgasm, making it more likely that she will gush when she comes. The Rainmaker is designed to do just that."

God, would I survive this man?

Xavier walked to the throne and retrieved a chalice, allowing the black silk laces to drape from his palm. "The king needed to make sure his queen was well-hydrated. His job was to see to her comfort." He held the cup to my lips. "She was given the most precious of gifts in the dry season—water. Drink."

The cool water soothed my anxiety-parched throat.

The doctor walked back to the throne, replaced the chalice on the arm before returning to me.

Starting with my ankles the doctor bound each leg to a post. The formation of the V caused my legs to spread and my breasts to fall on either side of the beam that supported my chest.

The doctor tied my outstretched wrists to the beam, so that I was bound in position.

"Are you comfortable?"

Surprisingly, I was. "Yes."

"Excellent. I had this one custom made for you. As any queen deserves. The original is there in the display case." He pointed to a glass enclosure, just beyond the throne. The dark weathered wood and sharp angles made it look like a medieval torture device. The one supporting me resembled a fine piece of abstract art.

"Once ready, he presented her to the crowd."

Marco slipped the neckline of my dress down, allowing my breasts to hang free.

The doctor retrieved a gold, gem-encrusted bowl from a pedestal beside the throne.

"The king placed a jeweled bowl under his queen's wide spread legs, in hopes to collect the rain she made as an offering to the gods." The doctor lifted my dress, exposing me.

"You are delectable, Elaine. Swollen. Ready. Clench your

muscles for me. Let me see how hungry your pussy is for us."

My body obeyed him without my will.

"Marco. Sebastian. You are lucky bastards. If only…" The disheartened tone to the doctor's voice didn't escape me.

Marco stroked his cock, already at attention. "Don't I know it."

I swallowed hard.

Xavier moved in front where I could see him again. "The king then took his spot on the throne. He selected one of his chosen to start the ceremony. His queen must be prepared." He picked up a long package, wrapped in brown paper, from the table. He peeled back the paper.

"I also had this crafted especially for you. Just as the king would have his scepter made for his queen." A large, ornately carved staff, topped with a glass ornament shaped like a smooth phallus, rested in his fist.

The doctor handed it to Marco. "The king bestowed the honor on his chosen guards who would be the first to take the queen and she spilled her first drops symbolically for the throne."

Marco disappeared behind me with the staff. I felt something cold touch my wetness. I jerked against the bindings.

Xavier retrieved a bottle of wine and the chalice before taking a seat on the throne. "Marco is going to fuck you with the glass top of the staff until you cry out my name."

Before I could register the doctor's words, Marco thrust the large object inside me.

I gasped.

The doctor relaxed in the oversized piece of art, crossed his legs and sipped from the ornate cup. "Sebastian, I want you to stroke her clit. I want to hear her scream when she comes."

A moan escaped my lips.

Marco slid the glass cock in and then pulled it out, only to slam it back inside.

It was cold, hard and filled me unlike anything I'd felt before.

The doctor sat the chalice on the pedestal, reached down and opened his zipper as Marco continued to slide the glass cock in and out of my heat. Sebastian stroked me in time with Marco's thrusts.

Oh God.

The doctor pulled forth his shaft and it stood tall and hard. "Look at what you do to me, Elaine."

Marco sped up. In and out. Faster. Harder.

Between watching the doctor, the superb fucking from Marco, and Sebastian's fingers, I could barely breathe. "God..."

"That's it. Scream my name." The doctor gripped his cock.

Marco and Sebastian increased their speed.

"Fuck." It felt so good.

"Are you going to come for me, Elaine? Are you going to give me what I want? Do it."

"Ahhh...fuck..." I was coming. Hard. I threw my head back and my bound legs locked.

"Say it," the doctor panted as his hand worked his cock.

I ignored his command, while gritting my teeth from the intense feeling of the glass cock sliding in and out of me, and Sebastian's nimble fingers dancing on my clit.

He rose from the chair. His cock bobbed as he crouched by my side and fisted his hand in my hair. "Say. It. Who are you coming for?"

"You."

He pulled harder. "Who?"

"You, my king."

My orgasm seemed to last for hours as Marco's rapid thrusts coaxed gush after gush from my depths.

"Who do you belong to?"

Before I could think better of it. "You, my king."

"That's right. Never forget it."

My heavy breaths brought me back to my senses.

The doctor released my hair and I rested my head on the wooden frame, trying to catch my breath.

"Very good, my queen."

Marco removed the staff from my body and presented it to the doctor.

He lowered the glass end to eye level so that I could see and smell my sex coating it. "God, what I wouldn't give to bury my head between your legs. Just smelling you makes me want to come. Do you know how many pheromones are released when a woman comes?" He licked the side of the scepter, tasting me, and I almost came again.

"The town's men passed the scepter from man to man, smelling the queen's sex, spurring them to arousal. The king then watched as each of the town's men lined up to fuck his wife. Just like I'm going to let Marco and Sebastian fuck you. Would you like that my queen? Do you want their cocks inside you?"

I really wanted the doctor, but this was the only way. "Yes. But only because I can't have you, my king."

He pulled tight on my hair. "You don't play fair do you?"

"Why start now?"

"Marco…" The doctor issued his command.

Marco didn't need to hear anything else. He buried himself in me in one thrust.

The word 'fuck' echoed off the walls, as it fell from both our lips.

The doctor remained kneeling at eye level watching my face, while his hand stroked his cock. "Some argue this ritual was a way to help strengthen the royal family with some genetic diversity. And remember how I said they believed all healing came from women. It wasn't unusual for the town's men to suckle the queen when she lactated, hoping to cure their ailments. Her milk was caught in a bowl and offered to the gods. Sebastian, on your knees. Suck her nipples."

It was hard to focus on his history lesson while listening to Marco moan every time he slid into me.

"Think about what's happening. You've reduced three men to their most primal elements. You are being possessed. You are mine, but never think that all we give isn't for you." He paused.

All I managed were gasps between each thrust.

"Harder Marco. Make it rain," the doctor demanded.

Marco increased speed and changed the angle of his thrusts.

I maintained eye contact with the doctor, who was only inches away. I moaned and panted with each stroke of Marco's cock.

Sebastian's hot wet mouth teased and sucked my nipples until they ached.

I couldn't hold back. The tightening in my stomach led to a rush that filled my head as I came harder than I ever had.

Marco groaned, "Fuck...you're so fucking tight," but continued to work me until I relaxed.

Deep breaths brought me down from my high, but Marco didn't stop.

The doctor leaned in closer. "Oh love, that was beautiful. You know each orgasm just makes you hungrier for the next. Women are designed to be fucked, over and over again. Yet, there are few men who can come more than once without recovery. Your body knows what it wants. One man will never satisfy you."

Marco rammed into me hard.

I gasped.

"These ancient people, who made the Rainmaker, knew your ultimate design. They also understood the driving desire for possession. This ritual was about the king's sacrifice and the queen's gift. Only with the king's permission was any of it possible. You understand that you are mine, right?"

It was part of the role-play, but I wanted the words to be true. "Yes."

"Good Queen. You please your king," he breathed, his mouth so close to my lips while his other hand slid up and down his cock.

Marco grunted and said, "Do you know I've dreamed of this ever since I first laid eyes on you? I knew X had good taste but never imagined... Since last night when I buried my head between your legs, this is all I've been able to think about." Another hard thrust and his large cock left me deliciously full.

I bit my lip.

The doctor shifted. "Tell me how he feels inside you."

Marco pushed and held, stretching my depths. A groan echoed through the room.

I tensed my muscles and squeezed him.

He slapped my ass and bellowed, "Damn, woman. You just bear-hugged my cock with your beautiful little cunt."

"He's large, Doctor. I feel very full."

"Do you want him to fuck you harder?"

"Yes... Please..."

Sebastian pinched one nipple between his thumb and forefinger and teased the other with his tongue.

It was hard to focus on one sensation over another, but Marco didn't disappoint. He fucked me hard, using my ass as a counter balance. He grasped my cheeks as he slammed his pelvis into mine.

The doctor fisted his own cock lubricating his motions with the pre-cum evident on the tip. I wanted so badly to touch him. To stroke him. To make him come.

Small grunts left my lips every time Marco slammed into me.

"Can the queen make a request of her king?"

His hand grew tighter around his cock. "What do you ask?'

"I know the rules. You won't touch me. I obviously can't touch you. But will you come for me?"

"What?" His hand stilled.

"I want to taste you."

He stared at me as though I had asked him to dance like a chicken or something ridiculous.

"What's the matter Doctor? I thought we were lovers. Climax is part of lovemaking. If you can't share your body with me, let me at least have your orgasm."

Marco growled. "God, that is so fucking hot. Do it, X. Come on her face." A sharp deep thrust. "Fuck. You're going to make me come just thinking about it."

Marco's enthusiasm and anticipation brought me to the precipice. My muscles clamped down on him. Tremor after tremor squeezed and urged him. With a final growl he filled me—hot and wet. Another gush streamed down my leg, a mixture of our desires.

"Goddamn, woman you could kill a man." Marco sighed,

and thrust a few more times. "Ummmm… I might have to fight you for her, X."

"She's mine." His eyes were dark with lust.

"I know. But can't we keep her? Damn." Marco pulled out, and moved to the front of the Rainmaker. He stood watching the power play between the doctor and me unfold. His beautiful body and his glistening, spent cock were visible, adding to my enjoyment.

But my focus was on the doctor. "So Doctor, are you going to play fair?"

"You don't." He stood, gripping his rock hard shaft. "Never… Never has anyone ever made that request."

"It's a shame, because I bet you taste wonderful."

He groaned.

Marco egged him on. "Come on X. Come on her face, in her mouth. If you don't want her to give you head at least make her swallow. Fuck. I'm getting hard again." Entranced by our scene, Marco fondled his half-flaccid cock.

You would think I'd have had enough, but my body was dying to service the doctor.

"I should make Sebastian fuck your dirty little mouth." He moved closer until his cock was only an inch from my lips. "How can I deny my queen? Open your mouth."

I longed to run my tongue along the ridge of the head of his cock. He was so close, yet so far away.

"Sebastian, fuck her." He pumped his fist harder and growled, "As far as you are concerned, that's me in your pussy. Think of me fucking you."

I did as he commanded, nearly salivating from anticipation. It wasn't that I liked the taste of cum, but the doctor was a delicacy. No matter the flavor, his release would be sweet victory.

Sebastian needed no urging, he spread my cheeks, giving him even deeper access to my sex. He slid into me and moaned, "God…so fucking hot. Do it, X." He forced breath from my mouth with each penetration. He fucked me hard, fast and deep.

The doctor worked his shaft faster, gripping it harder with each stroke.

I looked up to meet his gaze. "Let me taste you, my king."

He jerked. "Oh, Elaine…my queen."

I bit my lip and whimpered in anticipation, before opening my mouth to receive his gift.

The first drop hit my tongue and I braced myself for all of it. Stream after stream of white sprinkled my face, lips and tongue. I came, shuddering from the erotic sight, Sebastian's rhythm, and the doctor's trust.

The doctor bellowed as he pumped his cock harder, milking every drop.

I swallowed his offering, careful to lick the remnants from my lips.

"Fuck. That's… Oh…" Sebastian's bared the brunt of my orgasm. "Fuck!" he withdrew and shot hot, wet cum onto my ass.

Still gasping from the euphoria that filled me, I was eye to eye with the doctor. One last boundary to push.

"My king, may I make one last request?"

"I don't know if that's wise." His gaze was so intense; it was easy to forget anyone else existed.

"Kiss me."

"What? No."

"Why? Surely, you've kissed your wife. I can't touch you. Where is the harm?"

He said nothing. Still searching my eyes.

Marco and Sebastian moved to the table, leaving only the doctor and me in the moment.

He leaned in closer, so slowly his movement was nearly undetectable.

When he was in reach I placed my lips on his and breathed, "Taste us. Our love making, my king." His lips began to move with mine giving way to a passionate rhythm. His kiss said everything his words could not. The man was filled with passion, but someone had bound him with invisible restraints. I was determined to set him free.

As our tongues touched, I was lost. I felt him in my soul. His lips, so smooth and soft, comforted something in me I didn't understand. It was like in that moment, all that I felt for him, which had evaded me, became clear. I had to save him from himself. Lingering nudges from reluctant lips, signaled the kiss' finale, but we embraced our unwillingness to break the connection. The truth was I wanted to devour him, but I would have to accept what progress we made.

His breath was hot and his eyes dark with desire. He breathed against my mouth, "Make no mistake, Elaine, I am a king. Kings command and conquer. They are brutal and uncompromising. You don't want a king. Face it; you came here expecting a saint."

I nipped his upper lip. "I had no expectations." My tongue slid along his lower lip. "But I pledge my fealty."

He pulled back and stared at me. Indecision marked his features. "You don't know what you are saying."

"I'm saying I surrender."

His mouth crushed mine. His hands clasped my face. All of the conflict I saw in his eyes poured out in his kiss. Hard and soft. Slow and fast. He communicated more in that kiss than his words could ever say.

Our lips parted. Heavy breath met heavy breath.

He held my face and issued his command. "Untie her. She has given more than the gods could have ever asked."

He stood and tucked his cock back in his pants, zipped up and turned. Without another word he left.

Marco worked on the laces that held my feet and Sebastian untied my hands.

What the...? "Where is he going?" Surely, after that... I sighed.

"He has a speaking engagement. You're stuck with Sebastian and me tonight."

Son of a bitch. Marco stepped into his pants, pulled them up, and then handed me a towel.

"Does he always do that?"

"I don't think so. I've never...participated before. But wow! So fucking hot."

I glared at him. "Not that. I mean, does he run when pressured?"

"Oh that." He chuckled. "No. X doesn't run from anything. I think though, he's never been as frightened as he is with you."

"I don't get it." I used, and then discarded the towel before repositioning my clothes.

"Come on. I'll tell you all about him on our adventure tonight."

I smoothed my hands down the back of my dress, making sure it was in place. "What does that entail?" I raised an eyebrow.

A cell phone beeped and Sebastian reached into his pants pocket.

Marco laughed. "Well, we promised we'd save the good stuff for X so...I guess we can take you sightseeing. Maybe we need to take you out for some steak. Let's just say, I haven't really been rehearsing much. I'll need some extra stamina for any more festivities like today. Damn."

Sebastian placed the phone back in his pocket and sighed. "I'm so sorry, but I'm going to have to take a rain check. Miriam just texted and she isn't feeling well." He grasped both of my hands in his and brought them to his lips and kissed one, then the other. "Thank you. X is a lucky man."

"It's no problem. Take care of Miriam." He gathered his things and left.

I sighed.

"Hey, being stuck with me ain't so bad."

I laughed. "That wasn't what I was sighing about."

"I know." Marco kissed me on the forehead. "Give him some time. He has a lot to process. Let's get you back so you can freshen up."

## CHAPTER EIGHT

# ENGAGEMENT

O N THE WAY HOME, MARCO POINTED OUT LANDMARKS and told stories of several drunken escapades that happened at some of the finer watering holes.

He had once spent weekends playing in piano bars while working his way through college and his dreams of being an international underwear model were squashed by the demand for his IQ.

He was fascinating, but I couldn't stop thinking about the doctor. Was he angry? Did I push too far? I understood abuse, but what drove him to his abstinence, even in marriage? The more I thought about it the more I needed answers.

My captive audience would be a good start.

"Did you know Lydia?"

"Yes. Wonderful woman. Beautiful. Very...very worldly. She had an elegance about her, but you always wondered if underneath she wasn't wearing a leather bustier. Sexy. Mysterious."

I ignored the pang of jealousy. I had no claim on the doctor. How would I ever compare with that?

Marco sighed, "There is something about a confident older woman. I mean that's why Sebastian married Miriam."

"Older? How much older was Lydia?"

"Well, X is thirty-four, so that would make her fifty-three."

"She was nineteen years older than him?"

He leaned over to grab a bottle of water and raised it to his lips. "Yes, but she didn't look a day over thirty. Lucky bastard."

"I'll have to take your word for it." Something about the story didn't feel right. I had assumed she was his age. "She was practically old enough to be his mother."

Marco leaned in as though he was afraid someone might hear. "You hear all these cases about female teachers seducing young male students and everyone gets up in arms. Lydia waited until he was of age, but they got married soon after X graduated med. school. Since he started university at sixteen he was a married man in his early twenties."

"I knew they met in college, but..."

"He signed up for one of her classes on sexual disorders. That's how they originally met. They got to know each other, she agreed to 'treat' him and that's when things took a turn for the unconventional."

"Isn't that against the rules? She was his psychiatrist, an established practicing psychiatrist, a specialist in sexual disorders and a professor at the university. How did she get away with that?

"She didn't. That's why they moved to Paris. The university asked her to leave."

"I'm really confused now. She was an expert. How did she not help Xavier with his...problem?"

The silence was deafening, as Marco leaned forward to stare out the window.

"What?"

Marco cleared his throat. "Do you want X's explanation

or do you want my theory? If I share it with you, you need to keep it quiet. Xavier wouldn't appreciate it."

"My lips are sealed."

He shifted in his seat and ran his hand through his hair. "I knew Lydia, but not well. Most of what I know is second hand from X. I made the mistake of suggesting once to him that perhaps the reason he never solved his problem was that there was no incentive for her to help. I mean, talk about having your cake and eating it too. Get to have two gorgeous lovers in private and hang on X's arm in public. He didn't take too kindly to my opinion and threatened to send me back to the States if I ever spoke ill of his wife again."

He had an excellent point. Why would you work to cure someone when it would do nothing but cramp your life-style? In her position, she had complete control. I had to know more.

"Was she vindictive like that?"

"No, she wasn't vindictive. But she was controlling and determined. She put her career above everything. And she used it to validate her sexual explorations. I have no proof that she was anything but a devoted wife who made a unique relationship work around her husband's limitations. And with her death we will never know."

"But you suspect something else?"

He nodded, "And Miriam suspected, too. One night at a party she had a little too much to drink and told me that she abhorred what Lydia was doing to X. She hasn't spoken of it since, but she saw it too. Speaking of Miriam, you didn't get to meet Charles, Miriam's father. He was shady as fuck. There is something strange about all that old French money—Lydia's family and Miriam's. Too many secrets."

Was it possible she never tried to help him? If so, how

could he not see it? Was it the age difference and her exper-
tise that made me suspicious? If there was one thing I'd
learned from my father, it's that if something feels wrong,
it usually is.

* * *

When we returned to the house, a long shower was in order.
My muscles hurt from the afternoon's activities and fresh-
ening was necessary. I wondered where the two of us might
end up. I would do my best to see if I could persuade them
to visit the Louvre.

The steam from the shower billowed through the doorway. I tied the belt to my luxurious robe and left my oasis,
while trying not to think too much on what I had done. Two
men. The doctor. I was pulled from my reverie by a knock
at the door.

Surely, Marco could give me this moment before
running me ragged all over Paris. I strode to the door with
a complaint on my lips, only to have it slip away along with
my breath. It wasn't Marco.

Xavier stood, head bowed, hands braced on the doorframe
in a full tuxedo. It was easy to forget just how powerful he
was, but seeing him like this left no doubt. The world sought
his attention. The vision in my doorway was that of the most
revered man in the world. After gathering my wits, and
clearing my parched throat, I managed to squeak out. "Yes,
Doctor. Is there something you need?"

"No." He continued to look at the floor.

"I'm sorry?"

He looked up. "It's not something I need. It's something
I want."

I swallowed hard. All the visions of the afternoon rushed
back. His lips. His taste. His trust. They quickly morphed

into a fantasy of him untying my robe and throwing me on the bed.

"I want you…" He inhaled and held his breath.

My heart thudded in my chest.

He continued, "To accompany me to my speaking engagement."

The invitation held promise but killed my fantasy. I did my best to hide my disappointment.

"Tonight?"

He righted himself and reached over and repositioned my robe over my nearly exposed breast. "Yes."

I would have given anything to read his mind. His responses were slow, deliberate.

"Sure. When should I be ready?"

He pulled back his sleeve and glanced at his watch. "In about an hour. Is that OK?"

"Sure, but Marco is going to be disappointed. He was looking forward to a night on the town."

"I'll break the news to him. I want you with me tonight." The intense stare returned.

"OK. "

"Oh and Elaine… The place will be crawling with media personnel. There will be a lot of questions, have no doubt. I'll do the talking, if you don't mind."

I hoped the reluctance in my voice didn't give the wrong impression. I was thrilled and terrified in equal measure. "Sure. Is this about my father?"

His eyes widened. "Oh…no. That's not the issue. It's just the last time I appeared in public with someone, things got out of hand."

"Oh, OK." The relief was hard to hide. I didn't want my father causing yet another problem for me.

He closed his eyes and took a deep cleansing breath. "I just want to make certain you understand what I'm asking. Until now…this moment…it can all disappear. No one will ever know that you were at my house. And you can walk away with no ties, no connection to all that we've done…and have yet to do. This changes our arrangement. There will be no denying our association. Although the details will remain our fond secret."

He reached down and picked up a bag at his feet. "Since you weren't expecting to be going to a formal occasion tonight…"

I was going to be Xavier Vincent's date. The only thing that could pull me from all possibilities the night held was the feel of his finger as he rested the bag's handles in my outstretched palm.

He closed my fingers around the satin cords and stepped in closer. "Are you sure? When this is all behind you and you are sitting in the conference room are you going to be comfortable explaining that it wasn't what they thought? Knowing that when you board that plane back to America, we go back to the way we were."

Disappointment killed my anticipation. I took a breath and swallowed my frustration. I'd treat it like a job, diligently plugging away and taking risks in hopes of a bigger pay off. There was something undeniable between us. But he needed to understand I wasn't fragile.

"Yes, Doctor. I'm fully capable of pretending to be your date, of enjoying this week, and then never seeing you again. You're not that irresistible." Yes, he was, but he didn't need to know it.

"Fair enough…" He paused. Cleared his throat and turned. As he walked away he muttered, "See you in an hour."

I closed the door. Not a moment to spare, but my mind raced. He had a point. It was one thing to have his attention when it came to sex, but this was something else. In a way, I was flattered that he wanted to be with me. There were few women who would turn down his offer, but there was a big difference between fancying a romp with someone and wanting to be seen with them in public. Hell, since this was a speaking engagement, there would be photographic evidence. I didn't want to be so excited, but I shivered from anticipation. I knew the chances of this living up to my expectations were minimal, but there was always hope. After all, he was the one who'd pointed out that I'd suffered enough to deserve it.

\* \* \*

After putting the finishing touches of makeup on, I had one final task—zipping the damn dress. A knock on the door startled me, but it could be serendipity if the knocker had two hands.

I turned the handle expecting to lay eyes on the doctor, but it was Marco and he was stunning. Black, slicked back hair, tuxedo and a mischievous grin.

"Hi beautiful, I stopped by to see if you are about ready."

The sleeve of the black, shimmery gown slipped and I pushed it back into place.

"I thought you'd still be headed out." The sleeve fell again.

"I asked X if I could tag along since you might need the company while he hobnobs." This time he caught the stubborn garment. "Turn around. Let me zip you up."

I did as he asked, thankful for his help.

"I need to tell you a few things." He pulled the zipper, running a finger along my spine, causing me to shiver. "Here let me warm you up." He wrapped his arms around me and whispered in my ear, "You're going to meet Roxanne tonight."

"Who?"

"Um… She's X's last love interest."

I tried to turn but his arms held me in place. "Stay here. If he knew I was telling you this, he'd kill me."

"I thought there hadn't been anyone since Lydia." I relaxed knowing that trying to force my way out of his embrace would be a waste of energy.

"Yes, well. That is true. Remember when he said he pretended to date someone to shut Sebastian and me up? That was Roxanne. But he got tired of answering questions. Roxanne works in a prominent role as a fundraiser for the Cancer Society. She's beautiful, but vicious."

"Wonderful."

"She was in love with X. Let me rephrase that… She was in love with the idea of him, but she didn't know him. He kept her at arm's length. She finally got tired of not getting anything but superficial public invitations and called it off."

"So this is what he does…" I couldn't hide my disappointment.

"Bella, no. Not with you. You are different. He trusts you. And unlike her, you love him as a man, not as an icon. "

"I do not love him. I find him fascinating."

"Call it whatever you wish, I know what I see."

I sighed. Lying to him wasn't fair; denial was my burden. "No, you're right. It just seems pathetic to fall in love with someone so fast."

"Well, if it is pathetic, you're not alone. And Roxanne isn't going to be pleased. I didn't want you to be caught off guard. And the other thing…"

"I don't know if I can handle anything else."

"He has a reputation that I… may have perpetuated for him…but long before you."

"What kind of reputation?"

"Let's say… You'd never know that he spends his nights alone. He's considered one of the most eligible bachelors of the country. So expect others to be vying for his attention."

"Oh great."

He squeezed me a little tighter. "But remember, he didn't invite them. He invited you."

He placed his lips on my cheek and whispered, "He has excellent taste."

"Can I be honest with you?"

He turned me in his arms, allowing me to gaze into his deep brown eyes. So gorgeous. Like a work of art. "Bella, you can tell me anything. I know that our meeting wasn't typical, but unlike Xavier, who is fighting an internal battle with his past and his desire, I'm not. If you want to keep in touch after this week, I'd be honored. But if you'd rather move on, I understand."

"Marco, that's the thing. I have very typical reactions in an atypical situation. I honestly don't know what I want. Is it even possible for him to love me? Would I be willing to love him if I could only have part of him? I so want to help him. Allow him to know true intimacy without reliving his past. But no one is ever successful at changing another person. If Lydia was an expert, and couldn't do it…"

He reached up and stroked my cheek. "Couldn't or wouldn't? I may not have known Lydia well, but it was obvious she adored X, much like a collector enjoys their prize artifact. She, like Roxanne, was in love with the idea of him. She was older and emotionally detached. She supported his career, but they led very different lives. I often wondered if she didn't perpetuate the problem. Then I watch you two. There is something between the two of you that wasn't there with Lydia."

"Lust."

"No." He thrust his hips forward, rubbing his rock hard cock against me. "No. This is lust. I have to admit X is a brilliant director and you are a most talented leading lady. It's wonderful, but that's not what you and X feel. When you kissed him today, it was loving and tender. You are the first woman I've seen that really wants to see him as a man and not a celebrity. That's the only thing that can save him."

"I just hope he wants to be saved."

"Every man does but will rarely admit it." He kissed me on the cheek. "Let's get you to your chariot, M'lady. Your king awaits."

## CHAPTER NINE

# REVELATION

T HE LARGE STONE BUILDING RESEMBLED A CONCERT HALL or opera house. Members of the media held cameras and protestors held signs, handwritten in French.

The amount of frenzy outside the hall was more than I expected. "What is the topic of the event?"

The doctor looked out the window. "It's a cancer research fundraiser."

He shifted so that his leg rested against mine. The electricity between us continued to grow. I was slowly becoming consumed by his every touch. It was not good. These feelings could never lead to anything productive. I tried to focus on something else. "What are they angry about?"

Marco leaned forward and looked out the window. "Oh, they are the animal rights activists. Even though Western has the most ethical and humane laboratory practices, many would love to see humans replace the guinea pigs. I can admire their conviction. Even if their tactics are sometimes tiresome."

The car parked and Marco exited, followed by the doctor. When he emerged, people applauded and cheered and blinding camera flashes filled the car. He offered me his hand, steadying me as I stepped from the car onto the side-walk. The cameras continued to flash as the doctor laced his fingers between mine.

I leaned in to whisper to him, but he raised our joined hands to his mouth and placed a soft kiss on the back of my hand—the gesture was so normal...familiar...loving...and public, that it silenced any thought I had.

A photographer turned to the rowdy crowd of protesters screaming various chants in French beyond a barricade of police. One emphatic woman stood out. Her haggard features and tattered clothes added to her intensity. From her mouth flowed in plain, American-accented English, "Murderer! Murderer! Murderer!" Anger and hate lined the woman's face as she struggled against the officer holding her back.

I whispered, "What is that about?"

He squeezed my hand gently, but said nothing as we made our way through the entrance.

The grand lobby of the hall seemed to swallow us. The huge, ornate columns and marble floors spoke of France's history. Gold leaf cherubs held plaster banners that framed the ceiling. I tried my hardest not to look like a tourist, but the place was breathtaking. A band played in one corner of the large space. Waiters dressed in tuxedos served drinks on golden platters, making their paths between the guests and the large mahogany bar, which sat opposite the auditorium doors.

Another kiss to the back of my hand. "Beautiful." His lips lingered on my skin.

I glanced around the room one more time before facing the doctor to answer. "Yes. It's gorgeous."

He pulled me closer, wrapping his arm around my waist. "I wasn't talking about the room. I was talking about you."

This was more contact than I had been allowed to have with him previously. Butterflies filled my stomach, not because of his touch, but rather the way he looked at me. It was different. There was hunger, just like always, but something beyond that—something I could easily drown in.

The moment was cut short by the arrival of a taller, gorgeous woman with angled features upstaged only by her ample bosom accented by an extremely low cut neckline. The black material hugged every curve of her body. But I could feel the tension inside me tighten when she grabbed Xavier's other hand and purred, "X, it's been too long."

She leaned in and kissed him on one cheek and then the other, pushing me out of the way to do so. The doctor shot me an apologetic glance.

"Roxanne… So nice to see you."

Roxanne? Son of a bitch. This was my competition. The only woman he dared to date since Lydia.

She grabbed his hand and pulled him to her and tucked his arm in hers. He released my hand. Another glance.

She turned to me and said, "Please, excuse us, Xavier has some unfinished business he needs to attend to."

She pulled him into the crowd, leaving me standing alone. Marco was nowhere to be found. I don't know what I'd been expecting. A fairy tale, maybe. Fucking hope.

The bar wasn't far away, so I weaved and excused my way through the horde of guests. I grabbed a glass of champagne and scanned the crowd for Marco.

A few more steps and I stopped. Near the band was a dance floor. Twenty or so couples swayed to the music—many of them quite experienced. In the center, with his arms around her waist and her fingers twirling his hair, danced Xavier and Roxanne. Groin to groin they moved with the music. If it had been anyone but Xavier, I would have admired the sensual nature of the dance, but instead, my blood boiled.

Had he been lying to me? Was this all a sick game? Had he known she would be here? Fuck hope and fuck champagne. I turned away from the scene and set a path for the bar stool.

I grabbed the hem of my dress, holding it in place as I slid onto the high leather seat. The bartender approached me, but everything he said was in French. So I held up two fingers in the form of a 'C' about the size of a shot glass and mimed the motions of tossing back a shot. He got the picture. He placed a glass in front of me and pointed to the array of liquors behind him. I didn't care. It just needed to act fast, because this was not the night I imagined. I pointed to an amber colored liquid. He poured it for me. Brandy. It would have to do. I kicked it back and allowed the burn to leach through me as I inhaled deeply. He held up the bottle and pointed to the glass. I nodded.

He filled the glass and I wasted no time. As the second shot left that delightful warmth in my belly, Marco approached.

"What are you doing? A beautiful woman should never drink alone. Besides, that's not even the good stuff." He took a seat beside me.

"So where have you been?"

He placed his lips to my ear. "Better question is… Why aren't you with X?"

I sliced my head toward the dance floor.

"Dear God, she is here. I hoped I was wrong but… What is she up to?"

"Humping the doctor apparently."

He wrapped his arm around my shoulder. "You have nothing to worry about from Roxanne."

Just then the two of them completed a move so suggestive, that it looked as though they might have sex any minute.

I shot Marco a disbelieving look.

He turned, raised his hand and French words flowed from his lips. Soon my shot glass was filled and he held up his own. "Bottoms up."

We simultaneously downed them; we even wiped our mouths on our forearm at the same time and inhaled deeply in perfect synchronization.

"Just relax." He patted my knee.

"Why am I even here? You could be introducing me to Paris's dive bars."

He laughed. "You're exactly where you need to be."

"I find that hard to believe." Xavier dipped Roxanne. Something tightened in my chest. It was hard to determine if it was all the alcohol or hope shattering from the inside out.

"He doesn't love her. She was a publicity stunt. You are the one he invited."

"Great. I can add publicity stunt, along with prostitute and Celtic Queen to my resume."

"Stop it. You are not Roxanne. He didn't bring you here to satisfy the media."

The doctor nuzzled Roxanne's neck. "I can't watch this anymore."

"You know that he's in love with you, right?"

I slapped him on the arm. "Don't say that. It's not funny. It's just sex."

"He'd be a fool not to be." He brushed a strand of my hair off my shoulder and his finger left a trail of heat. Marco was such a beautiful man and an excellent lover. My mind wanted to drown in the alcohol and my body wanted to drown in Marco. It was a dangerous combination.

"You want to leave?"

He grabbed my arm. "No, Elaine. I'm serious. You were all he talked about since the first time he saw you two years ago. He sought you out. He's different with you. Different than he was with Lydia. The way he looks at you—"

"But it doesn't matter."

"It does because you love him."

"It won't matter on Sunday." I sighed.

Fingers long, rough and masculine slid between mine. It wasn't Marco as his hands were visible on the bar. Another hand snaked around my waist and hot breath hit my neck. "I'm so sorry. I had a few loose ends to tie up."

Marco's smirk was hard to miss.

"So that's what they call it these days."

The doctor held himself tight against my back. And he whispered, "See, she doesn't even make me hard." He pressed his pelvis against my back. "But you... Come dance with me."

"Isn't that too much touching?"

"There are enough people here to keep everything in check."

He spun me on the bar stool and grabbed my hand, leading us to the floor. My reluctance slowed our journey.

A white-haired gentleman in a white suit jacket stopped us. "Dr. Vincent."

"Dr. Monte, it's good to see you." The two men gave each other a stiff handshake.

The older man's curls bounced as he dipped his head. His hand clasped mine and he placed a gentle but wet kiss on the back of it. I wanted to wipe my hand on my dress, but he wouldn't let go. He stared at me, but his words were intended for Xavier. "Do tell, dear friend, the room has been abuzz wondering who this beauty might be."

My heart raced waiting for his answer. Would he say colleague? Friend?

He wrapped his arm tighter around my waist. "This is my Elaine."

The old man's stare grew unnerving. He kissed my hand again. I tried not to show my shock at Xavier's words.

"Xavier, you are one lucky man." He released my hand.

"More so than you know." They both smiled. "Dr. Monte, if you'll excuse us, I want to get at least one dance in before I have to speak."

He gave a slight bow. "Doctor. Elaine." Dr. Monte turned and Xavier pulled me to the floor.

Once our feet were planted on the dance floor, he wrapped his arms around me and pulled me close. He was so warm, so tall, so…hard. His erection grazed my stomach. I looked up and met his gaze.

His eyes were dark. Not their usual blue. "I told you, she means nothing."

"If you say so. It's probably too late to tell you this, but I can't dance."

His arm pressed on the small of my back and he lifted our clutched hands.

Hips swayed to the music, causing a delicious friction to build. "You don't need to know how. Just follow my lead. It's just like making love. Close your eyes and let your body feel mine."

The temperature rose six hundred degrees with his comparison. God, he felt so good. The words kept echoing through my head, "My Elaine." I needed to stop. Nothing good could come of my conventional notions, but he felt so right. The scent of sandalwood and musk filled my nostrils as I laid my head against his hard chest.

The hand on my back rubbed and soothed. He sighed. "What's wrong?"

"Nothing is wrong. Everything is perfect. And unlike Roxanne," he wiggled his hips and rubbed his rock hard cock against my belly, "you have this effect on me, always." His hand dropped to my hip and rested on the curve of my ass. "God, I wish…"

"You wish what?"

"You don't know how badly I want to make love to you. To see you wake up in one of my shirts. To roll over and suck on your nipples, while I bury myself inside you. You make me want things that simply aren't possible. Things I have no business wanting."

I couldn't breathe. My mouth grew thick from nervousness.

"Why are you doing this?" Our bodies rubbed together, my nipples hard under the fabric; I wanted him as much as he wanted me. Probably more.

He dipped his head and whispered against my lips, "Because I need you to know how I feel."

"Why now?"

"Because it's safe. You're safe. Do you know how long I've wanted to kiss you? And I don't mean a kiss like the one from earlier." He shivered. "Just kiss you."

"No." But I wished he would.

"The moment I first saw you, I wanted you, but I wasn't ready. Lydia had just passed. I needed to believe that I would never love again…" He broke his gaze and cleared his throat.

What did he just say? Did he say what I think he said?

"Why did you wait so long to contact me?"

He spoke, but he didn't look me in the eye. "Because I wanted you too much. I can't do conventional. I've never known a normal life and you deserve one. But this burning inside wouldn't let go. Marco brought us a bottle of cognac one night and suggested I bring you to Paris for a week to get you out of my system."

"Do you think it's working?"

He scanned the crowd. "Yes and no. I'm delighted, but it's agony knowing this time must expire. It's only fair. I'm broken, Elaine. You deserve a whole man." He stared into my eyes and I realized we'd stopped dancing. "Speaking of unfair things... I so want to kiss you, but you'd have to answer questions when you get home. A dance you can explain away, but if I kiss you..."

Before I could tell him to damn the consequences, a man in a business suit tapped him on the shoulder and whispered in his ear.

He released our hands, but left his arm around my waist. "Come on, love. I have to get ready for the speech. You can wait backstage for me if you'd like."

It wasn't really a choice since he took my hand and led me through the crowd.

We followed several men in suits down a long hallway and through a set of large double doors. Cords and ropes hung from the rafters and black paint covered the walls.

A tall man, in his early thirties, approached the doctor, and straightened the doctor's bow tie. "Dr. Vincent. They are eagerly awaiting your announcements. And the protestors are all secured outside. We don't want a repeat of last time." He clipped a microphone to the doctor's lapel.

Xavier straightened his sleeves and adjusted his cufflinks. The man handed him a small cylindrical object with a button on top.

"Just press the button when you are ready to speak. Harry

over there…" He pointed to a heavyset man sitting in a glass enclosure. "He'll monitor the sound and make sure your video displays correctly."

"Thank you, Nathan. Thorough as always."

The chill from the air conditioner, the alcohol and my body coming back to earth caused me to shiver. I crossed my arms and stepped out of the way. In the background, the audience chatter buzzed through the air.

Xavier turned and took a step toward me. "One last thing." He bent and placed his lips on mine, gripping my arms.

The shock caused me to stumble and he steadied me and deepened the kiss.

Our lips parted and in that small instant I was no longer cold. His smile only added to the heat that engulfed me. "Wish me luck?"

I smiled back. "Good luck, Doctor."

"You've got to stop calling me that."

"Why?"

"It puts distance between us."

"No more than the distance between Paris and New York."

"*Touché.*"

Nathan wedged himself between us. "Doctor, you're on in three."

"Coming."

He turned and walked on to the stage. The crowd applauded. Not with the enthusiasm of a rock concert, but rather the appreciation one might experience at a matinee of *La Bohème.*

He began. "My esteemed colleagues, thank you for coming out tonight…"

A tap on my shoulder pulled my attention from the charismatic man who was bound to be my demise. "Ms. Watkins?"

I turned to see Nathan. "Yes."

"I am so sorry to bother you, but there is a woman in the hallway requesting to see you."

"A woman?"

"Yes… She's ahhh…in a wheel chair."

That didn't make sense. The only person I knew in Paris in a wheelchair was Miriam, and she was supposedly ill.

I walked down the corridor in the direction Nathan pointed. When I turned the corner, Miriam sat in her chair dressed in the most beautiful beaded gown. Her hair was draped in wispy braids. She was truly beautiful. I couldn't help but smile.

"Miriam, you look stunning." I lifted my gaze to the man pushing her wheelchair—the undeniably handsome Sebastian. I blushed thinking of things we did earlier.

Her shaky hands reached out for mine. "Sebastian told me everything. Thank you. No need for you to be timid."

With my hands caught between Miriam's cold ones I said, "I didn't know you were going to be here. I'm sorry; I would have looked for you. Sebastian said you were feeling ill. I hope you are feeling better."

"I am. It's quite all right. Sebastian spoke with Marco and when he said you were going to attend the fundraiser with Xavier, I asked Sebastian to bring me. I think Sebastian needs to see that I'm really okay with this arrangement." She caressed his hand and gazed behind her and up at her husband. "I'm not just OK with this, I'm encouraging you. I love you and only want you to be happy."

He patted her shoulder. "I know. It's just…" He smiled, but it didn't hide the pain and awkwardness of the moment.

Miriam returned her sights to me. "Dear Elaine, do try to get him to consider joining you again with the other men. I can already see a difference in him. It's not good for a man to go so long without intimacy." She smiled and added, "Plus, surprisingly, I enjoyed hearing what transpired."

I took a deep breath, and wished I could hide my red cheeks. Could things get any more bizarre? I struggled to find an appropriate response. I settled for, "I'm sure it will all work out as it's meant to be."

"No truer words, my dear. I saw you and Xavier on the dance floor. Speaking of changes…That man loves you."

I coughed. "No, you're mistaken. I go back home in a few days. And then, as far as we're all concerned, none of this happened."

She laughed. "I'm surprised you could say that with a straight face. Nothing will ever be the same. Not you. Not him. Not us."

"I'm sorry, but that's Xavier's wish…"

"I need you to make me a promise." She released my hand and reached between her leg and the wheelchair arm.

Making promises to strangers never seemed wise, but what choice did I have?

"I'll do my best."

"Take Sebastian home with you tonight. Make sure that he's exhausted so that he sleeps late." She winked and smiled a mischievous smile.

I glanced at Sebastian who stared at the floor. The casualness with which she spoke of Sebastian and I having sex made the strange conversation even more awkward. It was easy to see that he didn't share her enthusiasm for discussing the topic. Sex with Sebastian would have been easier if Miriam and I had never met.

"And second, Xavier can't know anything about this." She handed me a small envelope. "Elaine, have you ever loved someone so much that no matter how wrong they were, your loyalty made you blind?"

I had. My father. I'd defended him long after the investigation pointed to his guilt. Denial, the therapist said, was common among children of serial killers. "Yes. I know the feeling quite well."

"Did you ever come to terms with it? It's one thing to accept someone else's actions, but to realize you've lied to yourself..."

Years after his arrest, pieces to the puzzle started to come together. The late nights. His fetish for impeccably clean garden tools. The strange stack of mail I found hidden in his bedroom. I stayed quiet, never voicing my suspicions out loud. The notion that the signs were there all along, but hidden until just in time for his trial, made me sick. Twelve life-sentences. With a new one to be added annually, with each new victim he revealed. "Yes, I've done that too."

"Here." She handed me the paper. "I loved Lydia like a sister. More than a sister. I promised her that her secrets would go to her grave, but I saw him with you tonight and... He is a good man. Loyalty can sometimes make idiots of us all." She sighed. "Well...do with it what you want. I'm sorry to put such a burden on you, but I can't risk that it die with me."

Sebastian clutched her shoulder. She reached up and grasped his broad, masculine hand with her shaky one.

I looked at Sebastian, pleading with my eyes for clarification.

He shrugged. "I wish I could help, but she hasn't even told me what this is all about."

Miriam placed her hand back on her wheelchair control. "I hope you love him as much as I think you do." Sebastian moved out of her way and she put the chair in reverse.

"Who? Xavier?"

"Darling, it's called denial. You'll be angry for not realizing it yourself, but one day soon, you'll be the woman he always needed. Please, don't make a fool of me."

"It's not that simple."

She turned her chair so she faced away from me. Sebastian shot me a sympathetic smile and turned to follow her. Her words echoed off the marble. "It never is when it's love. Sebastian will catch up with you after he fetches the driver to take me home. Don't forget what I said."

I stood holding the small envelope, still trying to process what had happened, as the hum of her wheelchair faded.

Patience was never my virtue, but it wasn't the right time to look.

*  *  *

Applause echoed through the doors into the auditorium from the hall behind me. The note could wait. I couldn't squash the anticipation I had for seeing the doctor. The turn of events behind stage had my head buzzing. Where would it go? Could it be more? Did he have to be only a memory after this week? Dangerous, dangerous thoughts. I headed for the doors.

Before I reached them, Xavier emerged, his smile brighter than I had ever seen. He grabbed my hand and said, "Come with me."

His demeanor was so different than the norm. Perhaps the crowd energized him. He all but skipped, dragging me down the long hallway away from the crowd. He turned the corner and pressed my back into the wall. He engulfed my body with his. "God… Do you have any idea what you do to me?"

He didn't let me answer. He crushed his mouth to mine. So warm. So alive. His lips played with my lips while his body rubbed against me. His hips gyrated, pushing his swollen cock against my stomach. He trailed his mouth across my chin and down, until settling at the base of my throat—sucking and kissing. "I shouldn't let this happen. If you weren't leaving soon this would be dangerous, but as long as we are surrounded by people, we're safe."

Fire. I was on fire. I was too distracted by his heat and tenacity to ask what he meant.

"In another life, Elaine, you'd be mine. I'd never let you go. It's scary to think of what you make me feel and it's only been a few days." His teeth grazed my neck and his hand grabbed my breast and squeezed. His actions grew more frantic by the moment. I wasn't certain that we weren't going to end up fucking in the hallway.

"Why another life?"

His breathing labored and the spice of his cologne intoxicated me. He slid his tongue up my throat and nipped my ear before saying, "Because I can't give you what you need. I'm broken. I should have left you alone, but I can't."

"You're not broken, Doctor. You're a puzzle. Let me put you back together." It was time to push. Untie another one of his strings. I reached down and cupped him through his pants.

His body stiffened. He paused then locked gazes with me. "You don't know what you're asking. Besides, I'm afraid some of my pieces are missing."

"I'm a pretty good artist. I can draw you new ones." I squeezed his cock.

"Murderer!" A voice bellowed from behind me.

I released him. He turned, shielding my body with his. I leaned to one side to look. A woman, who looked to be in her late thirties, clutched a knife and approached us from the direction of the exit.

Xavier backed up, pinning me against the wall. "Annie, be

reasonable. Security will be here soon. Put down the knife. How did you get through?"

"Shut it." She poked the knife in our direction. "You have to pay for what you did." She shifted weight from one foot to the other and her mousy brown hair fell into her face.

"I have. Just not in a conventional way."

"Bullshit!" She blew the hair out of her eyes with a puff of air.

"Annie, I paid your family generously. You spent it on drugs. That isn't my fault." He grasped my hand.

"You killed her. You should be in jail."

"Maybe so. But that wasn't my choice."

Tears ran down her face.

"I wish you could find peace."

"Fuck you." She coughed gasping for air. The wheezing sounded painful.

"You're ill, Annie. Let me have my driver take you to the hospital."

"I don't want your fucking charity." She sniffled and stared at me. "He's going to kill you too. Just like my sister."

He squeezed my hand.

"Put down the knife," called out a security guard. Several burly men rushed in from the direction of the stage and surrounded her.

Her shoulders slumped forward and she dropped the knife.

She looked up from between the long strands of her stringy hair. "You ruined me. I fucking hate you."

"Annie, get clean. For the past decade or more, we've been through this. I keep atoning. I can't bring her back. But you can save yourself. I can't do that for you."

Two security officers grabbed her by the arms and pinned

her against the wall. She didn't resist, but continued to spew hateful words at the doctor.

Two officers who looked to be with the Paris police approached us. Xavier turned and wrapped his arms around me. "I'm so sorry. I never expected that to happen."

One of the officers spoke with Xavier in French, but he didn't release me.

"What did they say?"

"They asked if I wanted to press charges."

I rubbed his back, trying to sooth him. "And?"

He sighed. "No. I never do."

The sound of shoes tapping marble filled the hallway as they escorted Annie away.

Xavier released me and took a deep breath. "I'll call Pierre and have him take you home."

"If that's what you want." It wasn't what I wanted.

"It's not, but it's only fair."

I laughed, but the sound held a sarcastic edge. "See, I think fair would be you explaining what just happened, but to you sending me away is fair. Shutting me out every time things get uncomfortable, like how you left before I even dressed this afternoon. Or the best yet…making me believe you care when it's all just a game. If that's fair, and I stupidly allowed myself to forget the rules, then you'll have to excuse me." I turned and walked away from him.

"Stop! Can't you see I'm trying to protect you?"

I stopped and faced him. "From what? You? You're not that scary; I'm not that stupid and I'll never be a damsel in distress. Someone once protected me from the truth and you see how that worked out. I hate to correct you, Doctor, but hope isn't a gift, it's torture. And since you can't possibly save me from that, I have no choice but to save myself. If you can't share the truth with me then this *has* all been a game and I fold. Good night, Doctor."

I was tired of him running. The only way to stop it was to force the issue, hoping he'd follow to gain back his control. The irony of the situation was not lost on me. My stomach churned. What if he didn't? What if this was the last time I saw him? I turned back around and continued my exit.

"Where are you going?" he shouted, anger accenting every word until they echoed through the corridor.

I didn't answer. If he wasn't going to talk, I might as well see Paris. It was time someone stopped taking his direction. I increased my pace.

The bevy of patrons flooded the lobby and I weaved between them. I resisted the urge to look back to see if he trailed.

I pushed open the heavy iron doors and was greeted by cool night air. Where should I go, the Louvre? Better yet, the Paris Opera House; I had always wanted to see it.

Pierre noticed me and exited the driver's door. How serendipitous that he was still on site. He mumbled something in French and I hoped that the doctor's directive to take me wherever I wanted still stood. I was lucky that he understood me when I said 'opera house.' He opened the car door for me and I stepped inside. He closed the door and I buried my face in my hands, hoping somewhere deep down that all of Xavier's declarations were true and that this wouldn't be the end.

Pierre's door closed and the engine started. When the car pulled out my heart fell. At the end of the semicircular entrance to the hall the car stopped. The door opened, allowing a flood of cold air in, just before Xavier bounded through the door.

He slammed it closed behind him. Never looking at me, he faced forward and adjusted the sleeves on his jacket. His jaw was clenched tight.

He leaned back and ran his fingers through his lush hair. With sharp, crisp words he asked, "Where are we going?"

I cupped my hands in my lap. "I'm heading to the Paris Opera House. It might be closed, but at least I can see it from the outside."

He growled. "This is why your visit is only a week. I didn't want to have to explain this." He looked as though he'd aged ten years in the past thirty minutes.

"You don't have to. It's not my business." The movement of the car jostled me from side to side. I crossed my arms.

He rubbed his hands on his thighs. "No. No. It's not that. I just wanted this to be perfect. A week in time where the demons behaved." He stopped and turned to me with a penetrating gaze. "Is it wrong that I wanted you to see me for the man I want to be, not the one I am? I never wanted to see your face when you learned the truth."

"No, it's not wrong. But I realized back in the hallway, I have no interest in a fairytale. I had one of those and when you close the book, it disappears. I want you to trust me enough to let me know who you are. But none of it matters, it all ends soon enough."

"What if I don't want you to take this with you?" There was no humor in his tone.

"Was your plan to bring me here and make me fall in love with a character? Some fantasy you dreamed up? That seems cruel. Besides, far too many people have already done that. Don't you think it's time you find someone to fall in love with you? The flawed, real, imperfect you?"

He raised an eyebrow.

It was my turn to sigh. "Yes, Xavier Vincent, I know you're human. You pretend you're in control, but you're not. Your past is pulling your strings. If I were to fall in love, it would be with you and every tie that binds you. So what's your story? Just how understanding would I need to be?"

"No one is that understanding."

"Lydia had to be."

His eyes narrowed to a glare. I'd hit a nerve. That was good. If he felt the need to justify himself, he'd get to the point faster.

"I mean, she had to love you unconditionally, right? She knew all your secrets."

His head slumped forward and after a long moment, one where I thought perhaps I'd gone too far, he started on a whisper. "I was fifteen. And as with everything, I didn't do anything halfway, even then." He paused and released his hair, shooting me the most intense gaze. The moment of silence hung in the air thick with tension. "When I love, Elaine, it's with my soul. I love so deeply that I'm consumed. I'm like that with most things."

I was so dedicated to hearing his story; I didn't notice the car had stopped.

He looked up, and reached into his pocket and fished out his phone. "One moment…" A swipe of the screen, and a few number sequences later and he was carrying out a conversation in French. It had something to do with the opera house.

The door opened, he stepped out and then reached for my hand, "Come on."

I stared out the window at the ornate structure. "It looks closed."

"It is, but I'm a big patron. They are going to let us in." He leaned in, grabbed my arm and pulled, until I unfolded and gave him my hand.

Once outside the car, he laced his fingers with mine and led me toward the beautiful building. It was so large and opulent it was impossible to find words to describe. Sculpted, golden angels, supported by large stone pillars, stood watch over patrons from the rooftop. The street was quiet except for a couple laughing near a lamppost. Up a small set of stairs, under a stone archway and through an iron gate, stood large, gilded doors. One opened as we approached, revealing a dark-haired, fair-skinned man who wore blue overalls. Xavier spoke with the man in French and we slipped through the door.

All I could do was stare. Everywhere I looked, something to catch the eye. The echo of the man's footsteps died somewhere in the high gold leaf ceilings.

"Come on. I'll show you where I usually sit."

I was thankful he didn't want to continue our conversation as we passed through the hall of chandeliers or when we scaled the grand staircase. It was too easy to be distracted by our surroundings. But even with all the abounding beauty, I kept coming back to the feel of his warm hand holding mine.

More stairs and then finally a small corridor filled with narrow, brown doors, each with a small round window and gold lettering.

"This is it." He opened the door and revealed a small room with an opening to the theater. Red velvet chairs had been scattered haphazardly throughout the space.

The doctor moved a settee to the front of the box, just behind the intricate gold-leaf banister. His movement echoed through the cavernous empty space. The heavy, red curtains with golden trim obscuring the stage were not enough to absorb the sound.

He took a seat and patted the space beside him. "Join me."

I did as he asked and continued to stare across the massive room, considering the time and effort it must have taken to construct the building.

He grabbed my hand and squeezed it.

"Her name was Samantha. We were both fifteen. As I told you in the car, when I love I go all in." He focused his attention on me.

I smiled, trying to picture a fifteen-year-old Xavier Vincent. "Teenage love can be intense."

"No. You don't understand. It still happens." He didn't pause long enough for me to comment and even though we were alone, he whispered to reduce the echo. "Anyway, I was in love, but I was being pursued by universities for early admission. My test scores were off the charts. My parents were poor and uneducated, so they didn't understand the importance of what was happening. They just wanted to make sure they got their check and didn't owe anything. A guidance counselor at school was my advocate and I was enrolled at Harvard before my sixteenth birthday."

"Wow, so you and Marco have a lot in common."

He laughed. "I think that's the only point, but yes, I understand the struggles of early admission. He's much more of a punk than I was."

It was good to see his smile even if it only lasted a few seconds.

"I was afraid of leaving Samantha. I figured if we had sex and I was the one to take her virginity, she'd have a stronger reason to wait for me. Fifteen-year-old male logic at its finest."

It was my turn to chuckle. "It's been my experience that most men don't progress past that."

"Yes. I guess you're right. Only when they're older, they drag you off to Paris."

We stared at each other for a moment. Gazes locked. Why did I want him to say it? To tell me he loved me, when in the end it amounted to nothing more than something else that would haunt me when I was long gone from France.

He folded his hands in his lap and turned his gaze back to the elaborate boxes on the other side of the theater. "We had it all planned. Her parents would be away the weekend before I left. Even the timing of her cycle was perfect: I didn't want to get her pregnant." He cleared his throat. "Being teenagers, things were awkward. I remember fumbling with her clothes and penetrating her for the first time, the grimace on her face that turned quickly to a smile is etched in my mind, but I remember nothing after that."

"What happened?"

"Lydia diagnosed it as transient global amnesia brought on by orgasm. Basically, I lose memories before and after. Supposedly, I get confused too. But like I said, I don't remember any of it."

"Wait. Lydia diagnosed you? But I've seen you orgasm and you were perfectly in control."

"Hang on, I'm getting there." He sighed patted my leg with our entwined hands. "The next memory I have is lying naked on top of Samantha, my hands around her throat, choking her already lifeless body."

I gasped.

"I tried to revive her, but she was dead. I called 911 and when the authorities arrived, I was arrested. I still can't believe I did it. I loved her, Elaine. I never wanted to hurt her.

I didn't know I was capable of hurting anyone like that and especially not her." The sincerity in his voice broke my heart.

"I didn't fight the charges and my parents went on a campaign to get me convicted. You see my father had been sexually abusing me and was afraid I would expose him, so discrediting me protected him."

"Oh, my god. I'm so sorry."

His sarcastic laugh filled the hall. "I just told you I killed a woman while fucking her and you feel sorry for me. Don't. The reason Annie keeps torturing me is because she is right. I got off easy. And if you want to know what Samantha looked like, picture Annie at age fifteen, before the drugs and hard living. They were identical twins."

"How terrible that must be to keep seeing her face."

He turned to me, anger marking his brow. "Why are you doing that? There should be no sympathy for me. I didn't do a day of jail time. The same powers that paved the way for my education covered it all up. My parents gave up custody. I was adopted by the Lenoir's—a wealthy family with ties to the university. Samantha's family was paid off and no one ever spoke of it again. Except Annie. As guilty as I am of Samantha's death, I'm also guilty for Annie being collateral damage." He let go of my hand and clenched his fists. "Security assured me that they would be on the lookout for her."

"So that's the real reason you won't have sex with anyone?"

"Yes. I won't risk anyone else. There must be some kind of monster in me for that to happen, so I have to keep it in control at all times. That's why I don't participate and I always have at least one more person present. So if you want to leave, I won't stop you."

But he was not a monster. I knew what a monster looked

like. My father's despondent stare when he was arrested was unmistakably evil. He wore his role of father like a mask, but when it came off, there was no denying what he was. My father had always been perfect because it was a role. So stereotypical because that's what he needed to be. Xavier was too raw and unrehearsed to be hiding a demon. Regardless of what had happened on that night or whether he did real time or not, he had paid for his crime. "Xavier, look at me."

He did, but there was reluctance in his movements.

I searched his eyes for anything that hinted at deception, but I was met with grief, guilt, regret and fear in the red-rimmed eyes that refused to cry, but wanted to so desperately. There was no hint of what I'd seen in my father's eyes—neither the perfection nor the chaos. "I'm not leaving. I've seen monsters. You are not one of them."

"You can't argue with truth."

I placed my hand on his thigh. "You're right. You have a condition that caused a tragedy. You could have as easily been a narcoleptic and fallen asleep at the wheel of a car. You had no intent to kill her. A monster is someone who looks for a victim, chooses his prey and hides the bodies, all while eating dinner with his family every night and attending his children's soccer games. Just so when the headlines hit the paper, they can call him the perfect family man."

"Your father?'

"Yes, Daniel Simon Watkins, otherwise known as the Basement Killer. All of his victims were found bound and tortured in their own basements. And just to add a little interest to the game, he hacked off various pieces of them and hid them in random locations just to make the investigation more entertaining. He didn't stop killing. He'd still be arranging hunting trips today if he could. Yes, that sick bastard hid everything from us. That is a monster. Not you."

"I'm so sorry, Elaine."

I threw back his words. "Oh, don't feel sorry for me. Had I paid a little more attention, had I questioned a few strange coincidences, the toolbox in his car that didn't make sense, those women would be alive. I could have stopped him. But I was so wrapped up in what I wanted to believe that I didn't see the truth. I feel responsible for all of them."

He grabbed my hand and squeezed.

"I decided that day, the day he admitted to it all to save his life, to open my eyes. To watch what goes on around me. It was my sister who saved me. My mother was killed in a car accident when I was eight. My father played the perfect grieving widower. My sister is everything to me, and if you had gone to prison, if your life had taken any other course, she'd be dead. So forgive me, I don't mean to be callous, but I think you've more than atoned for your sins. You may have taken a life, but you have saved so many more. And most importantly, when I look in your eyes, I see nothing but compassion."

"Elaine..." He said my name as though it were an apology. "Now do you see why I wanted to let you go home?"

"I see why you made that ridiculous choice, but I still don't agree with it."

He turned sideways, facing me full on. "You can't be serious."

I returned his stare. "Why?"

"I just told you I murdered someone."

"And I just told you that my negligence lead to the deaths of countless women who were raped, tortured, hacked into pieces and left to die in their own basements. We all have our demons. It's all about whether or not you rise above them.

Besides, we all walk away, right? Secrets intact." I blinked and it occurred to me. "Wait. I'm sorry. Maybe you don't want me after learning the truth."

"Nothing could be further from the truth."

I leaned in just close enough that I could feel his breath, but not close enough to touch his lips to mine. "Xavier?"

He released his response on a breathy whisper. "Yes."

"I want to make something clear."

"Yes."

I inhaled and held my breath, slightly longer than comfortable. "I want you."

My lips collided with his. His hand clutched the back of my head, holding me to him.

"Fuck. Do you know how much I've wanted to hear you say that?"

I wanted to forget. I needed him to forget. Time was running out.

I glided my hands over his thigh and across to his zipper, and our tongues danced. I rubbed his length and he hardened in my hand; I squeezed and stroked with slow, seductive caresses.

He took long shaky breaths.

"If it were just the two of us...tonight...and we...we were uninhibited. What would you do to me?"

He moved his hand to rest on my breast and his lips peppered kisses along my neck. "I dream the same dream about you every night. I have since that conference where you delivered that idiot a hard dose of reality in front of everyone."

He nipped my neck with his teeth.

"The first thing I'd do is bury my head between your legs and lick you until you screamed my name." He pressed me closer to him. "Every time you're aroused...it's like my body knows and I can barely focus. You are not good for my concentration, Ms. Watkins."

"Are you saying that I'm standing in the way of medical progress, Doctor?"

"I should be focused on molecules and cells; instead all I can think of is how much I want to make love to you. I want so badly to make you come."

"Well, rest assured I have no intention of impeding medical progress."

I stood, hiked up my dress and slid my panties down my legs

"What are you doing?" He rubbed his hands on his pants.

"Consider it my contribution to science." I handed him the undergarment.

He rolled it up and placed it in his pocket just as he did in the restaurant earlier in the week.

"Elaine, I can't..."

I extended my hand encouraging him to stand. Once he did, I turned him, placing his back to the banister, reached up, and pressed down on his shoulders.

"What...?"

"On your knees, Doctor." He took the hint and fell to his knees.

"What if I hurt you? I couldn't live with myself."

I removed the long strand of pearls from around my neck.

"I don't think it's possible, but for your piece of mind..." I leaned forward and grabbed one arm and tucked it behind his back and then the other. I used the strand of pearls to bind his hands together. "There. Now you can't get your hands near my throat. But for what you wanted, you won't be needing them." I sat in the center of the settee and judged his reaction a moment. Shock laced his features. I then leaned back and bunched my dress around my waist. With a smile on my face, I spread my legs.

He groaned. "Oh God..."

"Come closer."

He scooted on his knees toward me.

I grabbed his head in both my hands and kissed him hard.

He released my mouth on a heavy breath. "But I've never..."

"You're a doctor. I have faith you know your anatomy." I spread my legs wider and pressed on his head, guiding him to where I needed him.

"Elaine... I can't believe..."

His five o'clock shadow left a delicious burn on my thighs. With the first stroke of his tongue, I shivered. That was all the encouragement he needed.

"You're so wet." He lapped and licked his way back and forth across my wet flesh, his nose nudging my clit with each upward motion. With every stroke, I grasped the back of the seat and pressed my pelvis harder against him.

"Oh God... Xavier..."

He paused long enough to say, "I love hearing you say my name." When his mouth contacted this time he sucked and licked from the very bottom of my slit until his lips closed over my clit.

"Fuck...so good."

He moaned against my skin, causing a soft, tantalizing vibration. I squealed and it spurred him on. His chin rested against my opening and applied pressure every time I moved against his face.

"Xavier, you're going to make me come."

He buried his face harder against me and focused his tongue's rapid movement on the very tip of my clit.

The vision of Xavier Vincent on his knees, hands bound in pearls, with his head buried between my legs with the Paris Opera House as a backdrop would always haunt me. But in this moment, it was the sweetest victory.

He looked up at me, his face glistening, and said, "Come for me," then immediately returned to his task.

I squirmed in the seat; the more I moved the harder he pressed against me. I would have never believed he was a novice.

With the flat of his tongue he rocked his face up and down, touching me everywhere.

I let go of the seat, grasped his hair and wrapped my legs around him. I came undone.

"Xavier… So good…don't stop." The rush filled my head and my body tensed. He pulled back just in time to capture the gush of desire on his tongue and he devoured it like a starving man.

Several more passes and he sat up, his eyes black with desire. He scooted between my legs closer to me. His mouth captured mine and drowned me with the taste of honey and musk. While our tongues danced, I reached for his fly and scooted closer to the edge of the settee. I slid the zipper down and reached inside.

He breathed against my mouth, "Oh Elaine…"

His height placed his cock in perfect alignment with my core but I wouldn't push him that far. I pulled him from his trousers and grasped him in both of my hands.

He peppered my face with kisses as I stroked his shaft. With every motion he moaned. I smoothed the pre-cum with my thumb and worked on setting a rhythm.

"Elaine… Oh God…I…"

With both hands I rocked him, stroking him with my

palms. He leaned forward and doing so allowed his cockhead to graze my sex each time he thrust forward into my hands.

"Fuck…" He bit his lip and leaned in further, causing the very tip of the head to enter me with each forward movement.

His mouth captured mine and his kiss was brutal as his hips pumped hard and fast into my fists.

He cried out, "Oh, Elaine. I'm coming. I'm going to come on your pussy."

The words still hung in the rafters after he threw his head back, pumped his cock in syncopated motions into my fists and sprayed his release onto to my sex, mixing it with the remnants of my own.

With the final thrust, he stilled. His chest heaved with deep breaths. I released him and sat back.

He stared at me, locking gazes. "How am I going to let you go?"

I didn't answer, but watched as he looked down to see his handy work.

"Untie me."

I leaned forward and removed the pearl strand that could have easily broken with a little effort.

He stretched his fingers, and then pressed on my chest urging me to sit back. His hands pressed open my thighs and he stared. With deliberate slowness, he reached out and touched me, sliding his fingers back and forth through the milky white streams. He pulled my hips forward so that I could see what he was doing from my angle.

"Elaine, do you know how dangerously close I am to falling in love with you?" He gathered the sticky liquid on his fingers and without warning, shoved them into me.

"Do you know how badly I want to come inside you?"

I was already hot, but his words, his fingers…damn.

His fingers worked up and down, teasing my clit and then slamming into me.

"It's not perfect, but…" Two fingers slid in and out of me. Watching them disappear inside me was the most erotic sight. "…I'm inside you, Elaine." He leaned forward and wrapped his arm around me, while maintaining the rhythm with his fingers.

"Xavier…"

"Yes. Should I fuck you harder?" he breathed in my ear.

"Yessss," I hissed with my head thrown back and eyes closed.

His hand sped up and several more thrusts were all it took. I quaked in his arms and my body clutched his fingers. He rocked his hand a few more time in and out until my body stilled.

"My queen?"

The words were almost impossible to utter through my desire-parched throat. "Yes, my king."

With his fingers still inside me, he whispered, "Do you love me?"

It wasn't fair of him to ask, but I wouldn't lie to him.

"God help me. I do."

He removed his hand and wrapped his arms around me and held me in silence for some time.

## CHAPTER TEN

# FIRSTS

E VEN LESS MADE SENSE NOW. HE WAS STUBBORN, BUT NOT impossible. On the ride home, he held me against him in the backseat of the limo, but he was eerily quiet and all I could focus on was that I was running out of time. He hadn't returned my declaration, so I was in this alone. "I have a question. How did you meet Lydia—I know you said she was a professor?"

"I took a class on sexual dysfunctions, hoping it would give me some insights about why I didn't remember anything. One day she mentioned vacationing in New Harbor, Maine. It was my home town before moving to Boston with my adopted parents, so I struck up a conversation with her after class."

"So, you were her student and she treated your condition?"

"Yes, but there wasn't much that could be done. When our relationship turned physical, she suggested our arrangement. I found satisfaction in it, so we made it work. One thing led to another and we were married two days after I graduated med. school, but we had been involved since I turned eighteen."

"So you started watching her when you were still in school?"

"For some reason, I don't black out from masturbation, so it worked for us." He shifted in his seat.

My mind whirled. I still couldn't reconcile how this much older woman, an expert in the field, could supposedly treat his condition without helping him more.

"So obviously, she didn't have sex with Marco. He was probably at third grade band camp. So did she pick new partners or stick to the same ones?"

"One was always the same, Charles—Miriam's father."

I tried to keep the shock from my face. Marco had said he was 'shady as fuck.'

"Their parents had been family friends and he was a professor at the same university. Charles was her inspiration for studying psychology. He and his wife were divorced and after discussing my case, he agreed to help."

"Well, that's very hospitable of him." Sarcasm laced every word. "So he was always one of the participants?"

"Yes, but it all matters little now, they're both dead." It was impossible to miss the defeated look that overshadowed his features.

With a soft pat to his leg to express my sympathy I added, "I'm sorry she wasn't able to help you."

He shot me a glare. His brow furrowed. "What do you mean? She gave me a chance at something."

I needed to tread carefully. Failing to see her nobility was my issue and obviously an opinion I alone held. But could I make him see? Did his loyalty make him so blind that he didn't see the significance of what he had just done?

"And it wasn't for a lack of trying. Charles was a memory specialist. He worked with PTSD war veterans trying to manipulate memories to alleviate their symptoms. He tried to help me too. It didn't work."

"I'm sorry. You know what…? Enough of this heavy talk. Tell me what you had planned for tonight before I foiled your plans."

He laughed. "Even though I may not have enjoyed your methods, I did enjoy the end result. I have to say I am a little disappointed that my plans didn't pan out. It was something I think you would have really enjoyed." He hugged me tighter.

I smiled. "At least now I can say I saw two landmarks after a week in Paris. But what did you have in mind?"

He locked gazes with me. "I wanted to watch Marco and Sebastian fuck you at the same time."

It was the perfect opportunity to untie that final string. "Call them."

"What?"

"I only have one more night to ruin you for all other women." I smiled. "Unless you don't want to?"

He stared at me and retrieved his phone. He swiped the screen and touched something. I heard a quiet ring. It was a man's voice that answered, but it was too faint to make out who it was. Xavier spoke in French to the mystery voice. Never taking his eyes off me. He pressed the button.

"They are going to meet us at the house."

\* \* \*

Pierre stopped in front of the house and the doctor threw open the door. "Come on." He laced his fingers in mine and pulled me from the car. His brisk pace made me unsteady. He was so excited—like a kid at Christmas. He fumbled with the front door.

"So you had to speak with them in French so I couldn't understand you?"

"Yes." The smug expression showed through his attempts to hide it.

The doors opened. He yanked me inside, and then pushed the door closed.

With the click of the latch, I was pinned against the wall. His mouth demanding entrance to mine again. Passion.

He stopped for a moment. "If you must know. I called to make sure they were here." Another kiss. Hot. Rough. The feel of his five o'clock shadow left a delightful burn. "I want to fuck you so bad. You can't even understand. I ache for you. The taste of you in the theater only made me want you more."

I started to speak, but he placed one finger over my mouth. "What I have planned for you is so much better." He pressed his swollen cock against me.

"Where are we going?"

"Upstairs. There is a glass observatory overlooking the gardens. You can see Paris in the distance and it is a cloudless night. The stars are brilliant."

Dear God... Could I survive this?

"I have one condition." I tugged on his jacket.

"You can't make demands. Remember, I'm your king." He kissed me behind the ear.

"I could always retire to my quarters."

He gasped. "You wouldn't."

"I will if you don't meet my demand."

"Demands. This must be serious. What is it your heart desires?" He reached up and played with a strand of my hair.

"I want you to keep kissing me through all that's about to happen. Please."

"God, Elaine. I lov—"

He was interrupted by Marco's bellow, "Hey, X, we're up here."

Son of a bitch. What had he been about to say?

He stepped back and looked at me and shouted, "Coming."

We climbed the main staircase and strode down the main hall in record time.

At the end was a spiral staircase that led up to a beautiful glass paned observatory. The lights of Paris twinkled in the distance and the stars winked back, but as I stepped into the room I became keenly aware that I was the prey. My predators—three gorgeous men in tuxedos. Marco and Sebastian stood with their backs to me, hands clasped in front of them. With each slow step, Xavier following behind, my heart raced and I prayed I didn't start to sweat.

Marco turned around. He held out his right hand. I walked to him and placed my left hand into his.

Sebastian turned and grasped the other, flashing a brilliant smile. They each raised my hands to their mouths and placed a soft kiss to the back.

Xavier placed his hand on my hip. "Let them love you for me. Let them show you all the pleasures I can't." He placed a kiss to the back of my neck, and then hoisted himself up onto the edge of a black wrought iron table formed of ivy and flowers.

Sebastian reached behind me and unzipped my dress. They eased it over my shoulders and let it fall to the ground. Marco unlatched my bra and it slipped off with ease.

Sebastian cupped my breasts while Marco eased my panties down my legs.

Xavier called out from his seat, "Doesn't she have the most beautiful breasts?"

Sebastian cupped one and flicked his thumb over the nipple. "Yes."

Marco smoothed his hands over my hips. "Elaine, you are exquisite."

I turned to face Xavier, dislodging the men's roaming hands from my body for a moment. I grabbed each of their hands and walked to the doctor and stepped between his legs. "If you love my breasts, then show me."

He stared at me, but didn't move.

"Touch me, Xavier."

My nipples were hard and my body burned with sexual energy. I released the men's hands and cupped Xavier's face. "I don't know where the line is, but you touched me in the theater. Make love to me, Xavier. Give me all of you."

His hand grasped my breast. His eyes turned dark. "Marco…is she wet?"

Marco slid his fingers between my thighs and through my heat.

"She's dripping."

The doctor traced slow circles around my nipple—teasing and pinching. I nearly combusted.

"Sebastian, get on your knees and tease her with your tongue." He raised a hand. "But don't give her what she wants until I tell you. Marco, prepare her."

Sebastian wasted no time. He dropped to the ground, placed his hands on the inside of my thighs and coaxed my legs apart. With the first touch of his tongue, I shivered.

Marco's long finger slid into me, and the feel of all three men touching me made my legs weak.

Xavier lifted my breast and closed his lips around my nipple and sucked.

God. So good. So fucking good.

Marco inserted a second finger and increased his pace. The wet sounds coming from Sebastian's tongue and Marco's fingers echoed off the glass.

I moaned.

The doctor sucked harder, while flicking the other nipple with his thumb.

I placed my hand on his thigh.

He sucked hard.

I inched my hand toward his cock; he didn't waver.

Marco withdrew his fingers and to my surprise spread the wetness across my puckered hole. I tensed.

The doctor released his hold on my nipple. "What's wrong, Elaine?" His eyes grew wide with concern.

"Ahh...I've never done..." Marco rubbed a circle around the tight skin.

"Marco will be gentle. I told you that there is no greater pleasure than to be taken by two men. The female body was designed to be shared. Men are impatient."

"One condition." I leaned forward so that I could whisper in his ear.

"What's...that?" His voice was husky and rough.

"It has to be you."

He stared at me.

I inched my hand further up his thigh.

"You know I can't."

His cock was hard under the fabric and I placed my hand on it and rubbed and squeezed it.

He moaned.

"It feels like you can. And you did just fine during your test run." I winked.

"It's not a lack of ability..."

"What if I told you I trust you? There is no risk with Marco and Sebastian here. If you won't accept that I trust you, then trust that I know what I'm asking." I leaned in to seal my proposal with a kiss.

"God...this wasn't the plan."

"Wasn't part of your plan…" I rubbed him hard through his pants. "I seem to be good at ruining your plans."

"Fuck."

Marco pushed his thumb into my wetness and withdrew it. His fingers slid back into place and his thumb pushed against my muscled entrance. One push and he worked past the resistance.

I gasped.

"Marco, stretch her. I don't want her feeling any pain."

I glanced down for a moment, locating his zipper. A second later, I pulled it down. "Tell me what not to do."

"You shouldn't be doing any of it." His features held conviction, but he didn't move to stop me.

"And I shouldn't be allowing virtual strangers to fuck me on a rooftop in Paris. This week is all about breaking rules." I reached into his pants, parted the opening in his boxers and grasped his cock.

He groaned, "Elaine."

"Yes, that's right. It's me. And Xavier…" I was careful to use his name. I needed a connection. "If I'm going to lose my virginity in a sense, I want it to mean something. It has to be you."

"No offense, Marco and Sebastian." I glanced back at Marco who was rocking his fingers in and out of my ass and pussy, pulling down stretching the hole. Amazing. I'd never imagined it would feel so good.

"None taken. I'm perfectly happy being your fuck toy." Marco laughed.

Sebastian added, "I don't think you understand just how lucky you are, X. Most men have to beg for what she's offering you."

"So, what's it going to be?" I stroked him, sliding the

pre-cum down his length. "Are you going to fuck me or not?"

"X, she is just what you needed. Listen to her," Marco chimed in from behind.

I grabbed his face and stared into his eyes. "This is about us. About me giving myself to you. Are you going to reject me?"

He didn't say anything, but reached for his belt. His fingers clasped the buckle and undid the clasp.

His glassy, dark gaze held me. "Marco, lay down on the floor." He scooted to the edge of the table. "You... Take Sebastian's cock into your mouth. If your mouth is full you can't make any more demands."

He was always a slave to everyone else's passion. I'd pushed him, now it was time to give him control.

"Yes, my king."

He reached up and grabbed my head, winding his fist in my hair, and crushed his mouth against mine. Hot. Brutal.

He pulled back. Placed a soft kiss on my lips. "Get." Another one. "To it." He released my hair and pushed me toward Sebastian, who was already stroking himself from base to tip. His erection stood tall and thick.

I swallowed the head and slowly licked the underside of his cock with the tip of my tongue. He still wore his tux; I grabbed his cock in one hand, so I'd have better control when he came. He closed his eyes and moaned. I slid my mouth further down his length, inch by inch, savoring the feel of his smooth shaft. He was a large man and with each stroke of my mouth my jaw ached a little more. Marco's cock greeted me and I let go of Sebastian's with a pop and opened my mouth and engulfed his head, stroking up and down before alternating between the two men. Every time I engulfed one of them, their chest rumbled.

Marco placed his hands on my head, urging a faster pace, "Oh, damn…so good."

Xavier moved closer. "Elaine, you are so fucking beautiful." He walked around us, taking in my performance from three hundred and sixty degrees. He was a predator. He was the alpha, a position denied to him by circumstance and compassion. But I would ensure the king claimed his throne.

He stopped. "Marco, get undressed."

Marco withdrew from my mouth and I turned my focus to Sebastian. Out of the corner of my eye, I watched as the doctor and Marco undressed. It wasn't time to declare victory but…

Sebastian rocked his hips and I held still and allowed him to set the pace as he fucked my mouth. There was power in the act. Trust and control.

Marco and Xavier stood naked. Both hard. Both gorgeous.

I sucked harder, urging Sebastian as he pounded into my mouth.

The doctor pushed back on my shoulder and caused Sebastian to fall free.

"Marco, on your back."

He complied and laid his back on the tile floor.

"Elaine…" The doctor turned me toward him and kissed me. His naked cock touched my belly. "Take that beautiful pussy over there and fuck him." He kissed me again. "Finish off Sebastian, but don't swallow."

"Yes, my king." He assaulted my mouth with his. After several moments he released me.

I straddled Marco. "You are gorgeous, Marco," I said as I grasped his cock and placed him at my entrance.

"I know. You think you've seen perfection when you see

my face, until you see my cock…" He lifted his hips, slipping the head inside me.

"And so modest."

"I just call them like I see them." He smiled. "I mean, after all, I'd have to be pretty damn hot to have a beauty like you riding me." He leaned up and kissed me. "X, you are one lucky bastard. If you two get married, I better be invited to the wedding night, and I'll live up to my title of best man."

Sebastian nudged my lips with his cock and I sucked him in. "Fuck you, Marco, I've known him longer. If anyone's getting an invite it's me." He threw his back and set a frenzied pace. "God…Elaine… This feels so good."

"Guys, if Elaine ever agrees to be my bride, she'll get to call the shots, not the two of you."

Weddings? Brides? What the fuck?

Marco derailed my train of thought as he thrust into me hard, causing me to fall forward, releasing Sebastian. I caught myself with my palms before I crushed him.

Marco wrapped his arms around me. Holding me to him. He pulled out and said, "X, she's so fucking wet. But you might want to grab my jacket and check the pocket, I've been thinking all day about Elaine's little virgin ass and figured I'd better be prepared."

The doctor leaned over, grabbed Marco's jacket and wrestled a bottle of lube from the pocket.

Looking forward, I saw Xavier's reflection in the glass; his hand reached between my legs and they nearly gave out. Something touched me. He paused for a moment, and then slid his fingers back and forth between my folds. Marco withdrew and put his arms around me, urging me to lie on his chest and expose myself to the doctor.

Xavier dipped a finger into me and I almost came. He ran

his fingers over my sticky, wet sex. He took the mixture and covered me, lubricating my rear entrance in my own wetness and then dripped a cool liquid in the place I most needed it. He placed the bottle back onto the table.

"X, make sure you fuck her pussy first, it will make it easier on her." Sebastian moved forward and placed his cock at my lips again. "I want to be in your mouth while I watch Xavier fuck your ass."

The doctor paused. "Are you sure you want this, Elaine?"

"Yes, my king."

"We can't go back." His fingers traced back and forth between my two openings.

"I know."

With a sweep of his hand he gathered more of my moisture and coated me in it. A moment later his cockhead teased my entrance.

He reached and threaded his fist in my hair. "I want to hear you say it. Tell me you want me to fuck you."

"Fuck me, Xavier. Do it." He slid into my pussy and stopped.

"Fuck...you feel good." The doctor pulled out and thrust back in. "You're so wet."

Sebastian stroked his cock and nudged my lips with the head. "Wait until you're in her ass, X. Even hotter, tighter."

A few more strokes and he withdrew. He pressed on my hips, urging me onto Marco's cock. Marco gasped.

The doctor's hands grasped my cheeks, helping to slide me up and down Marco. He placed a hand on my back pushing my chest against Marco to expose more of my ass.

When the head of his cock touched my rear entrance I nearly came undone. I never imagined he'd give in. I never imagined I'd be excited for sex like this.

He gripped my hips. Riding Marco's cock, I set a rhythm,

while engulfing Sebastian with my mouth. In the reflection, the doctor stroked himself with one hand and kept the other one firm on my hip.

The thought of having him taking me that way sent me over the edge. I forced my clenching muscles down over Marco's length and released Sebastian's cock with a pop. I cried out, biting my lip as I rode Marco hard. Trying to get him as deep as possible, while grinding my clit against his pelvis.

Marco yelled, "Son of a bitch. So hot."

I threw my head back, gasping for air as my thoughts resurfaced.

Marco ran his thumb across my sensitive breast.

I shivered.

"Oh, X, you are in for such a treat. She's really tight after she comes. God…" He groaned. "She feels so fucking good." He continued to thrust up into me. "Lean forward. Let him take your ass."

Marco was still hard and buried deep inside me. I leaned down, resting on his chest. He rubbed my back. "Relax. When he enters you, breathe out. It will only hurt for a moment. And then you'll be amazed."

In the glass, Xavier placed his cock between my cheeks. "Tell me who you belong to, my queen."

"My king, I am yours." I held my breath heeding Marco's advice.

"Prepare to be mine."

"Elaine…" There was pressure as he pushed past the ring. He was a large man, so he took it slow. He stilled my hips. I took a deep breath. More pressure. A slight sting. A pop. With just the head in, he paused. "Oh God… Elaine. You are so hot, so fucking tight. Are you OK?"

"More than OK," I panted.

He pushed inch by inch until he was buried to the hilt. "Fuck."

Full, so full. The feel of both men inside made me dizzy.

Marco kissed me softly on the lips and then said, "X, you're in the driver's seat."

Sebastian commanded, "Love, open your mouth and let me back in." He kneeled beside me and slid his cock between my lips.

"I've gotta move." Xavier pulled almost out and then thrust back in, forcing Marco to slide back and forth inside me at the same time.

The doctor grabbed my hips for leverage as he moved with quick thrusts within me.

Marco bit his lip. "Hell, X, I can feel your cock."

In and out.

Hard.

Fast.

Sebastian grasped my head and sped up to a frenzied pace. "That is so fucking hot. Every hole filled. I can't... Fuck." He pulled out of my mouth and shot cum all over my back. The warm wet pools slid to the floor while the other men's assault continued.

Xavier and Marco both were spurred by the act. I watched the doctor grimace and gasp in the reflection every time he buried himself in me.

Sebastian pumped his cock, dripping the last drop of seed onto the tile floor.

Marco yelled, "Play with her nipples, Sebastian. I have to feel her come with us both inside her. Have to. Come for us, Elaine."

Sebastian leaned down and rolled my nipple between his finger and thumb.

Marco thrust into me, determination lacing his features.

The doctor cried out, "Elaine. You're so tight. So hot. I'm inside you." He stilled. "Fuck, Marco."

I was so full. It was unlike anything I had ever felt.

I rocked back against the doctor. He set the pace as he slid in and out of my ass. Faster and faster. Sebastian sucked a nipple into his mouth.

It was my turn to scream, "Xavier!"

Faster.

Harder.

Xavier held my hips like a vice and pounded into me.

Marco grimaced. "X, you're killing me. I'm going to come soon."

Quick hard thrusts.

He leaned over me wrapping his fist in my hair pulling back my head.

"Elaine, you are mine. No one else unless I say. Do you hear me? Once I claim you, you are mine. Say it."

"Yes."

He tugged harder on my hair. "Yes, what?"

"Yes, my king."

"Yes. Perfect." He thrust hard and deep.

"I'm going to come inside you, but first..." The doctor met my gaze in the mirrored glass. "Come for me, my queen. Give me all of you."

His words set me on fire. My body clamped down on both of them and they both cried out, "Fuck."

My release flowed over Marco's thighs and the doctor bellowed, "I'm coming, Elaine. I'm coming inside you."

Marco groaned. They both grunted and glided in and out in sharp, syncopated thrusts. They thrust hard, burying themselves as far as they could possibly go, and held there, the men pulsing deep inside and filling me with their last drops of release.

I stilled as they did and savored the fullness and the feel of both men. Xavier was right. There was nothing like it, but he was the secret ingredient. It wouldn't have been the same had it been Sebastian and Marco. It was his surrender that made the evening all that more delicious.

Marco was the first to speak. "That...that... Holy fuck!" He placed his hands over his eyes and let out a deep breath.

The doctor caressed my hip. "No words."

Sebastian tucked himself back into his pants and zipped.

I could barely think straight. It was, without compare, the best sex of my life. But beyond that was the satisfaction that the doctor hadn't blacked out, tried to kill me, or failed to perform. It all added to my suspicions. If any experience would have caused him to succumb to his amnesia it was that one.

Xavier withdrew, but his hands never left my body.

I rolled off of Marco and squealed as my back hit the cold floor. I sat up and Xavier wrapped his arms around me, holding me to him.

Marco stood and yawned. "Damn, woman. You wore me out."

I laughed. "I wasn't the one calling the shots."

The doctor kissed my forehead.

Sebastian walked over to me and bent to place a soft kiss on my cheek. "Thank you. I don't know that I can ever repay you."

"I would say the pleasure was all mine but..."

Xavier's arms were warm and he stroked my hair while he held me.

Marco picked up his pants and stepped into them. He

threw his shirt over his shoulder and stuffed his tie into his pants pocket. "Come on, Sebastian, I'm heading to the kitchen. All this sex makes me hungry." They walked to the door. "We'll meet you two downstairs."

The doctor warned, "Marco, don't eat all my bacon."

He laughed. "Don't worry, I'll give some to Sebastian." With that he disappeared.

The doctor grumbled.

The moment of truth.

"So..."

He cut me off with a kiss and adjusted me so that I sat in his lap, legs straddling him. "Elaine, I..."

"Shhhh...there's nothing to say." I placed a soft peck on his lips.

"But there is. I feel so much. So much uncertainty, so much hope, so much love."

I looked away from him. It was too late for me. I loved him and I knew that if I found myself on a plane when this was all over, it would crush me. I couldn't listen to him speak of love.

"Why don't we get dressed?"

"Elaine?" With a finger on my chin he guided me back to meet his gaze. "What's wrong?"

"Nothing's wrong. In fact, there's quite a bit right."

"Then why are you in a hurry to leave me?"

I placed my palm on his cheek. "I don't want to leave you." Never was there a truer statement. But it was hard to breathe. "I just think that you should consider celebrating your success."

"What makes you think I'm not right now? I have the most beautiful woman in my arms, one I just made love to. The ultimate prize for my success."

I smiled and tried to hide the pain. "We should go get

cleaned up. It's getting late. Didn't you say that you have to spend the morning at the office tomorrow?"

"Yes."

I leaned forward and placed another soft, lingering kiss on his lips. "Then let's get you dressed. And we want to be well rested for our last day together, right?"

The silence that hung in the air spoke volumes. He released me, but didn't dispute the timeline. My heart hurt that much more. I unwound myself from him and gathered my clothes. He did the same.

Pulling on his pants, he paused. "Elaine?"

"Yes." I pulled my hair loose from the back of my dress and turned my back to him.

"I can't stop thinking about what you said at the theater. About loving me. I can't think about anything else."

I couldn't look at him. Hell, I couldn't breathe. I took a deep breath.

"Well, then it's a good thing that I'm leaving soon. I wouldn't want to be known as the woman who ruined the great Xavier Vincent's plans."

"You already have."

"I would say I'm sorry, but I'm not." I backed up so he could zip my dress.

His finger blazed a trail up my spine and he placed a kiss on the back of my neck that made me shiver. I let go of my hair and turned.

"That's what I love most about you. Your honesty. How you risked everything for the truth." His lips captured mine, and our mouths danced.

I buttoned his shirt—one by one—savoring the feel of the light dusting of hair that cushioned his undershirt. Our lips parted with reluctance. "I think we end up valuing what we went the longest without. I spent my whole life in the dark. Never knowing that as my father chewed his prime rib, he was plotting the dismemberment of a stranger. When I'm weak I sometimes wish that he had never been caught. I know that makes me a terrible person."

He backed away a step and tucked in his shirt, then grabbed his jacket and tie and wrapped his arms around me. "No, it doesn't make you a terrible person. It makes you a grieving person. You're grieving for the life you knew. Trust me; grief can make you feel terrible things. But have no doubt, in those defining moments, someone of your character will always choose the noble, yet more troublesome path." He squeezed a little tighter. "Come on. I think there is champagne downstairs. We could both use a nightcap." He took my hand in his. It felt so normal. So real.

He was bound to destroy me.

## CHAPTER ELEVEN

# SECRET

T HE MORNING LIGHT WAS A RUDE AWAKENING. NOT ONLY was I tired and deliciously sore from the night before, but I woke in the guest bed. After the second glass of champagne I'd rested my head against Xavier's shoulder and that was the last thing I remembered. But I had hoped with the strides he'd made that I'd at least end up in his bed.

After the revelations and the previous evening's events, I had to find out what Miriam had gifted me. Why had she been so edgy? I retrieved the small purse I'd used the night before and pulled out the envelope. I tucked my finger in the seam and tore an opening. Inside was a paper, the size of a business card with what appeared to be an address, and a key.

I got ready in record time and after noticing that Xavier's coat was missing from its usual spot near the front entrance, I figured it was safe to leave. But I had no idea how to summon the driver. I opened the front door and stared directly into his chest.

"Oh, I'm sorry," escaped on a gasp. Not that it mattered, he couldn't speak English.

He smiled.

I reached into my pocket to retrieve the envelope and

handed him the card with the address. "Can you take me here?" I pointed to the card with 125 Toret, Paris written on the front.

He nodded his head in affirmation, turned and opened the door for me.

I climbed in and spent the next hour dreaming about all the wild things the secret might be, but anything fascinating was erased by Miriam's nervousness and her talk of a burden.

Sometime later the driver stopped outside Lydia's Gallery. I checked the address on the card and the numbers and the words on the street sign. This was the place. But why here? Surely, she didn't give me the smuteria as a gift.

I exited the car and again gave the driver a thank you. He may or may not have understood. The handwritten address couldn't have been penned by Miriam. Her hands were too shaky.

After taking in the new window display of modern erotic photography, I opened the door to the gallery. The sound of door chimes announced my arrival. Patrice looked up from her newspaper from behind the reception desk. She smiled and gave me a cordial, "Bonjour."

I returned her smile, nodded and busied myself searching the exhibits for any clue. Did she want me to find a painting? Was it stolen goods? Why the hell I was here?

A framed notice behind glass showcased some kind of greeting written in French, but it was the signature that caught my eye—Lydia Vincent. The signature matched the writing on the card. This was about Lydia, not Miriam.

The memories of the Rainmaker kept interrupting my concentration as I searched. I found myself gazing at the painting of the angel once more. The cage, his clipped wings and the woman standing over him, deserved another moment of admiration. The lifelike details and the vibrant reds against a black backdrop gave the scene of an angel losing his freedom a gothic, foreboding feel. It was hard to look away.

Exhibit after exhibit and none that required a key. The stairwell was clearly marked and the basement was my last hope. The fire door squeaked and gave way to a stone and mortar stairway. Concrete formed the path up, but down was everything you expected from a creepy Paris basement. Good thing the sex was good, because basement diving in Paris, instead of visiting the Louvre, was pathetic. Just another sign that I should probably let whatever Miriam's burden was, remain a mystery. I prayed there wasn't a dead body or something horrid like that.

I took my first step onto the stone floor and stood between the units made of wooden frames and chicken wire labeled one and two. Various artifacts littered the walk path. I searched up and down the main aisle for anything that might match the key. Lydia had a ton of stuff. But nothing. Who did Miriam think I was, Sherlock Holmes? Worried Patrice might find me rummaging in places I wasn't supposed to be, I hurried back upstairs.

I nodded to Patrice, whose welcoming smile was now a suspicious glare. The tinkling bells sounded as I walked outside, assessing whether I should give up or perhaps ask Patrice, or find a way to get in touch with Miriam.

I pulled the key and the note card from my pocket and looked at them again. The key had '1b' etched into the metal.

Up the hill was a building, attached to the gallery, which looked to contain small apartments. Could that also be 125 Toret? An ornate, large front entrance and many balconies adorned the structure. I climbed the stairs and on a door directly in front of me was 1b.

I wondered if the doctor had enough clout in France to expunge my record, should I get arrested for breaking and entering. The key slipped into the lock and the door opened easily. It was an office.

There were two desks, complete with two computers and two leather high back chairs. The walls were covered in charts and graphs, broken up with the occasional erotic painting. There were also several bookcases filled with books. The one window overlooked the gallery.

From where I stood, the handwriting on the desk blotter matched the writing on the card—Lydia.

Why would Miriam send me to Lydia's office? A mug sat on the desk and the dark brown stain in the bottom had long since been coffee or tea. The newspaper on the desk was three years old. The furnishings were covered in dust and in the far corner of the room a stain on the ceiling revealed water damage. No one had been there in a long time. There were still crumpled up papers in the trash.

What was this all about? I walked around the desk and there was a photo of a beautiful, young, Lydia. Strange… Why would she have a photo of herself? I moved to the next desk and upon it sat a photo of a young Xavier on his wedding day. The age difference between the two was striking. His smile was bright and naïve; it was nearly impossible to believe that this man, less than a decade later, had made the largest advancement in Cancer research ever—a definitive cure.

I pulled out the chair that faced the door and started looking through the papers on the desk. Nothing of interest. On the bookcases were dozens of notebooks in custom binding. I picked up the first one and a newspaper clipping fell out. *Youth Pleads Guilty to Murdering Girlfriend*. The article went into details of Samantha's death from strangulation. It was Xavier.

I opened what could be best described as a scrapbook and began to read. Thankfully, Lydia wrote in English, but the disturbing thing was that there were journal entries that corresponded with the date of his crime. He'd said he hadn't met her until college. What the fuck?

I laid the book—much like a parent might make for a child—on the desk and read entry after entry. Every detail of his life was noted, even those as a small child.

Hours passed and I was engrossed in a tale with fewer victims than my father's but no less devious. I skimmed notebook after notebook, stopping to take in the details of the horror story. I felt sick to my stomach and my head cloudy from shock. Inside a black leather journal found in the back of desk drawer, I found the most damning evidence. I grew sick from each chilling excerpt.

*Fucking Charles. "Maintain the integrity of the project," is what he always preaches until he gets himself in a bind. "Keep your distance." Is what he told me last time, but now when it's his fat in the fryer, rules are meant to be broken. Why does it have to be my subject? Can't he pick someone else? If I could kill Charles, I would. He has controlled me since I was a child when he would sneak into my room late at night. I'd kill him not only for that, and for getting me into this bloody awful Society, but also for all of the sick, twisted perversions his mind constructs. I'd be doing the world a favor to rid it of that sociopath. He killed that girl. He knew she was X's girlfriend, and that bastard had to kill her and now he wants X to take the fall. He'll pay for breaking his own rules. I'll make sure of it.*

Dear God... Miriam's father, Charles? The Society? Lydia knew Charles killed Xavier's girlfriend and never told him. That bitch!

*Charles calls it conditioning. That's how he explains his choice to place Subject X with those horrid people. I wish I had been able to follow X's case from the beginning, but let's face it, Charles only brought me in to lighten his case load. I'm safe since he feels he has control of me. I had always suspected the family abused X, but hearing the tales of what his father did to him made it real. I doubt Charles would see it as a tragedy since one abuser usually defends another. When I'm indignant about his decisions, Charles is always careful to point out that this is exactly why the "no contact" rule exists and by breaking it I only caused my own suffering.*

What in the hell were they doing? Playing games with people's lives. So that was why she never slept with him. She was keeping her distance. She perpetuated all his nightmares.

Rage. Burning rage bubbled through me. Lydia was lucky she was already dead.

*This afternoon I stood in the doorway to X's study and watched him devour the knowledge from document after document. It's been months since he started this fool's errand. When he placed his hand on my cheek, and told me he'd give up everything to save me from the cancer, I almost confessed. But what is the kinder path? I didn't make him a subject. I inherited him and my only solace is that I tried my best to salvage even the smallest amount of normalcy for him. I married him to give him every opportunity— access to my family's money and my constant oversight. But the decision is coming soon, if he doesn't reach his 'potential' before thirty, he'll be executed. I can only hope the cancer takes me first.*

What the fuck? Execute him if he doesn't reach his 'potential'? Who the fuck were these people?

*I'm getting weaker every day and the cure still eludes X. Charles had to die before I did. I couldn't allow him to ever tell X. I refuse to allow him to hurt anyone else. If nothing else, I am an unsung hero for ridding the world of Charles Lemiux. X is the closest thing I've ever known to love; I can't bear for him to know the truth. Charles and Miriam are the only people who know my secret. Miriam is loyal to the core, but Charles was enterprising.*

It was my only moment of smug satisfaction in the horrible story I had just read: Miriam's betrayal.

She continued, *it should only take a couple more doses to finish him off. Lazy man should have gotten his own coffee.*

She'd killed Charles. I eyed his coffee cup sitting on the other desk. This was their office. They were a team. Always had been. Xavier had been manipulated by two people who held the title of Doctor. What did I do now? Miriam wasn't kidding. This was a burden I didn't want. I had fallen in love with him just in time to crush him. Son of a bitch. I slammed my hand down on the desk.

My heart filled with hate. I was happy he didn't get a chance to save her. How could I save him? Should I keep these secrets to myself and carry this nightmare back with me to the States or should give him the truth? Fuck.

I had to leave. I couldn't take any more.

I placed everything back where I found it and I locked the door on my way out. The sun hid behind heavy clouds signaling the threat of rain. The limo sat outside the gallery, waiting. I walked down the stairs and directly to the limo door, but the driver wasn't there. I turned around just in time to make eye contact with Xavier, standing in the doorway of the gallery. His instant smile broke another piece off of my heart.

Several large strides and he threw open the door. "Elaine... You had me so worried. Are you all right?"

I nodded, but it was a lie. I wasn't fine. I couldn't let him know so I tried to keep my features under control, but the urge to cry stung my eyelids and tightened my chest.

He reached into his pocket and pulled out something shiny that reflected the sunlight. Before I could register his movements he wrapped his hands around my back and clasped the shiny object to my neck.

"Let me see." He lifted and held in his hand a pendant that hung from a silver chain. "It's perfect. That jeweler is a true artist and he made this in record time."

In his hand was a small wire cage with a pair of detached wings sitting inside. Just like those in the painting of the angel who had been forbidden to fly away.

"It is beautiful." I blinked my eyes, fighting tears.

"It's how I feel, you know. Like you freed me."

"But the door was open all along."

"You're right, the angel thought he had to fly to escape, but if he leaves the idea of his wings behind, he can walk out as a man."

I wiped the escaped droplet from my cheek. Could I get away with not telling him? If I really left tomorrow, was the truth worth destroying his world? I should throw away that key. Let him keep his love.

"Elaine, what is wrong? I didn't upset you did I? I just wanted you to have a memento. I'm sorry."

"No. No, it's not that."

Part of me screamed inside to walk away. It would be the kinder thing to do. Or would it?

The more the decision raced through my head, the more I couldn't contain the emotions.

He wrapped his arms around me and held me tight. I savored the feel of his embrace and cursed myself for teetering on the verge of a breakdown when he was the one who would be destroyed.

"I love you, Elaine. It wasn't part of the plan, but I do."

I was wrong. Neither one of us were going to make it out alive.

The tears flowed from my eyes. Why did life have to be so unfair?

If he truly meant it when he said he loved me, then I had to give him a choice.

I wiped my arm across my face, clearing the tears.

"Elaine, did you hear me? I said I love you."

Could I speak without hyperventilating? Was the truth worth throwing away any hope of love with him? Regardless, my love for him was great enough to let him decide. I refused to be another Lydia.

"Xavier, if you were me and your father had a terrible secret that would turn your life upside down, take you away from everything normal you'd ever known, would you want to know? I had a happy childhood, you know. That monster was a wonderful father. But to learn of the monster meant I had to lose my father and the illusion of my life. If you were me and you had a choice, would you choose to know or not to know?"

He kissed my forehead. "This wasn't the response I was hoping for when I told you I love you. I guess it depends on how much you value truth."

"And you... Do you value truth over all else?"

"Yes. I'm a scientist. A cure is nothing more than a discovered truth. An action to get the desired reaction. I spend my life seeking truth."

"So, you would give up the fantasy?"

"Elaine, what happened? How did you end up here? Patrice called me to tell me you were here and acting strange. As soon as my meeting ended, I came."

"Thank you, but could you please answer the question?" I sniffled.

He brushed a stray piece of hair out of my face. I should have been mortified, losing my composure, but the pain I felt for him was too great.

"I'd want to know the truth."

I couldn't hold it back. The words burst forth. "You didn't kill Samantha."

His features soured. "That's sweet of you to say, but I was there, Elaine."

"Yes. You had sex with her, but you didn't kill her."

"Elaine..."

"Just hear me out." I knew I sounded hysterical and by the look on his face, I must have looked it too.

"It was Charles. He killed her. He had been molesting her as a child."

"What?" Anger brewed behind his confusion.

"It was his hypnotic suggestion therapy—he merged two events. There were two separate instances. You slept with her. But you were placed on her dead body. They drugged you. They knew as a juvenile, you'd never go to jail. They let you take the fall."

His brow furrowed and his eyes narrowed. I would give anything to never see him this way. Never see the pain he was about to feel. "They?"

More tears gave way. "Charles and Lydia."

"That's impossible. Why are you doing this?" He backed away and crossed his arms.

"I debated telling you. Part of me wanted to leave and never have to see this look on your face. God. But I love you and I have to give you a choice."

"I didn't meet Lydia until I was in college."

"I know, but she knew who you were. Your adoption, the early admission to college, it was all part of the plan. They wrote the screenplay for your life to meet their needs and documented all of it. It was an experiment. It was Charles who drafted the production and Lydia perfected it."

His arms crossed tighter over his chest.

"But don't worry, she got Charles before she died. She poisoned him."

"Elaine, none of that happened. Let's go get you some help..." He grabbed for my arm.

"No."

I turned and raced back up the hill, pulling the key from my pocket.

"Elaine... Please..." He chased after me.

I stomped up the stairs. I placed the key in the door just as his arms circled around my waist and started dragging me away from the door.

"Elaine!" This time he shouted, anger pouring from him.

It didn't matter, the door gave way and I fell through the door, pulling him with me.

I bumped the desk and the coffee cup of death clanked against the table.

"It's all here. Every detail. Right there in those books."

His anger dissipated, replaced with bewilderment as he stared at Lydia's photo sitting on Charles's desk.

The tears returned and I realized that dealing with an angry Xavier would've been easier.

"I'm so sorry. The last thing I want to do is hurt you." I walked to him and grabbed his arm.

He remained silent, shifting his gaze around the room. He didn't acknowledge me at all.

I let go of his arm. A few steps later, he stared at his

wedding picture, as though he were trying to recognize the people in the photo. He picked up and examined it with careful scrutiny. His words were far too calm. "How did you know about this place?"

"Last night, Miriam gave me an envelope and a cryptic message about not being able to carry the burden. She said she could see that you loved me."

I had hoped that would have provoked some type of affirmation of his earlier declaration, but nothing.

"I didn't know the address was the same as of the gallery. Xavier, I am so sorry." He set the photo back in its place and pulled out the chair, moving almost in slow motion. His face revealed no expression.

"Xavier, I love you. No matter what you find…"

He didn't look at me. "Elaine, I think I need some time alone. You can have Pierre take you back to the house."

I covered my mouth with my hand to trap the escaping sob. "I'm sorry."

He didn't acknowledge me. Instead he opened a drawer and began sifting through the contents. I pulled out the key and the information written by Lydia and sat them on the desk. His eyes scanned my actions but he went back to his task without comment.

I turned and pulled the door shut behind me, clutching the necklace he'd given me in my hand.

I ran to the bottom of the hill. Pierre was waiting. He opened the door for me and mumbled something in French, which I took as question—Would Xavier be joining us? I shook my head, but he pulled out a cell phone to confirm.

Moments later he opened the driver door and started the engine.

The rain poured and there was nothing that could ease the heartache I had for the doctor...and me. Once more I had sacrificed everything I loved for truth. And all I could think—was it really worth it?

CHAPTER TWELVE

# CONTROL

LIGHTNING FLASHED THROUGH THE LEADED GLASS PANES of the large sitting room that opened to the foyer. The place it all began, what felt like a lifetime ago, but had only been a week. Pierre started the fire in the oversized hearth before he left me alone. It was that time of year when the days ran hot and the nights cold. The rain only added to the chill. After soaking in the spa tub, I settled into an oversized chair in the great room. I pulled my robe tight over my nightgown and waited for Xavier.

My stomach ached from nerves and I worried I'd never see him again. Would he blame me? The messenger didn't always fare well. Would he hate me for telling? Or would he simply be too embarrassed to face me? Either way, everything was over. I waited, legs curled under me, and a cup of tea in hand.

Too preoccupied to read or do anything else, I had fallen asleep and was awakened by a loud thud and a cold breeze. I jumped out of the chair, knocking over the china cup, and made my way to the door.

Xavier kicked off his rain soaked shoes. His drenched hair plastered to his forehead and his clothes were soaked.

I moved behind him and grabbed the collar on his jacket, urging it over his shoulders. He didn't say a word.

I expected him to push past me to undress in his room, but he continued there in the entranceway, leaving the clothes in wet heaps on the floor.

I helped undo the buttons of his shirt. He neither asked me to stop nor encouraged me. Inside, I wept with happiness for his return and in sadness for the pain he felt.

In one final tug, his boxers hit the ground and he stepped out of them. He stood naked. It wasn't the time to admire how truly beautiful he was, he needed comfort.

"Let me go make you a cup of tea." I turned, but he yanked my arm, pulling me back to him. With me held tightly against his chest, he walked forward, forcing me to stagger backward. The backs of my legs hit the couch and he leaned over me.

He reached for the belt on my robe. His lips brushed my neck as he pushed the robe off my shoulders. He groaned, but said nothing else. Backing away, he turned me until I leaned over the back of the couch. Was he going to fuck me? Was he testing his limits? No matter what he needed, I would be there for him.

Hands cupped the outside of my thighs and grabbed my panties at my hips and dragged them down my legs.

His hand slipped between my thighs, spreading my legs slightly. A finger slipped between my folds. If he was testing to see if I was wet, he wasn't disappointed. His cockhead pressed against my warmth and with a grunt, he buried himself inside me. I heard him suck air through his teeth before he stilled.

He pulled out then slid back in. But that was his only moment of hesitancy. He thrust in and out, then leaned over me so that the sounds he made in his throat echoed in my ear. He pushed on my shoulders every time he entered me. This was his catharsis. We weren't making love; we were affirming he was alive.

His movements grew frantic and he pounded harder, burying himself to the hilt on each thrust. I moaned at the power in his hips and how deep I felt him like this. His lips latched onto my neck and he sucked and kissed as his crescendo grew.

Soft gasps escaped my lips with each impact.

I held onto the back of the couch, weathering the storm that was Xavier. He cried out and with one last, deep thrust he held and pulsed with release—jerking and filling me with each shudder. He didn't move for some time, staying still inside me. His heavy breath and the crackling fire were the only sounds.

He pulled out, and turned me to face him. He took my hand and led me up the stairs and down the hallway. He paused in front of the room I stayed in, but continued on.

Around the corner were two large double doors. I squeezed his hand tighter as he opened them. The biggest bed I had ever seen sat on the far side of the massive room. A claw foot tub took the corner of the room. He pulled me gently into the room, until I stood at the foot of the bed. The thin straps of my gown slid from my shoulders, and then he picked me up by my waist and sat me on the bed. He mounted the bed, prowling toward me, and urged me in the direction of the headboard.

I worked to steady myself as he stalked toward me.

"I'm sorry," he said as his mouth covered mine.

He pushed me back and opened my legs.

I didn't fight him. He ran his fingers back and forth

through my wetness. He slipped a finger into me and with his thumb, held me open for his inspection.

He added a second finger and began driving them in and out of me. He moved up my body, with his hand remaining between my legs.

He pulled his fingers out and brushed them over my clit and then buried them in me once more.

He moved faster, resting his palm against my clit. He dipped his head and wrapped his lips around one of my nipples. He sucked and flicked his tongue across the tip while he rocked his fingers in and out. He shifted and encased me with his body. His movements became fast and deep, as he buried his face in my neck and kissed his way from my shoulder to my ear.

He increased the pace. Faster and faster he fucked his fingers in and out of me. He shifted his angle so that he reached deeper and hit just the right spot.

My legs stiffened. I grasped his back hard, digging my fingers into his skin.

His mouth covered mine and he swallowed my scream.

Through gritted teeth I moaned as euphoria embraced me. My back arched; I clutched him tighter and felt the flood of liquid escape.

His fingers still moved fast, but they made wet sounds every time he entered.

"Xavier…"

He placed soft kisses all over my face as I came back to earth, then one lingering kiss on my lips. He jumped out of bed, pulled back the covers, and covered me with them, before climbing in beside me.

He held me against his naked body and let out a sigh.

I reached up and touched his face. Asking why he was

upset was pointless. I wanted to know what this all meant. Did he need to forget? What would happen tomorrow? So I said nothing, but gave him comfort with my touch.

He wrapped me tight in his embrace as though I might get away. I savored the feel of him.

He ran his hand through his hair. "It was all a lie. I'm such a fool."

I cupped his face. "You're not a fool. You were a child. They took advantage of a child to explain away their own depravity and to play their sick game. You're not a fool. You're a victim."

"I've never been a victim, Elaine. I don't know how to be one."

"Then don't be one now. Don't let them win. Don't let this break you." I kissed him softly.

"I was broken before. I feel like this time, I shattered."

"I'm willing to help pick up the pieces." I grabbed his hand, then held and kissed it. "You know, and please, don't hate me for saying this, but had your life been any different, my sister would probably be dead, along with a thousand more, and more in the future. You can't change what happened, but you can choose what happens now."

"I can't stop thinking about it. About how I should have known."

"I can understand. I still have the same thoughts about my father."

He locked gazes with me—so much turmoil behind his eyes.

Now was the moment of truth. Did he mean what he'd said when he said he loved me, or was it something he just didn't understand?

"Shhhh... Let's not waste any more time. My flight leaves in the morning. Let's leave the past in the past."

He lifted my leg over his hip and slid into me.

The surprise must have shown on my face, because he paused. "Are you OK?"

"Yes, I guess I wasn't expecting you to be...ready...so soon."

He laughed and thrust in harder. "Don't get used to it. I think my body wants to make up for lost time with you." He kissed me.

I wrapped my arms around his neck as he rocked in and out of me.

Small groans escaped his lips along with sighs of contentment.

He increased his pace and buried his face in my neck. I moved my hand to the small of his back and caressed the muscles that tensed and relaxed with each penetration.

He nipped at my throat. "If only I had met you in another life..." Moan. "I could have been..." He held me to him as he shook. "Oh God... Elaine... I wish..." He released on a shiver and groan.

"Shhhhh...we can talk about it tomorrow. Just savor it."

He placed soft kisses along my jaw and wrapped his body around mine. "As my queen demands."

## CHAPTER THIRTEEN

# DEPARTURE

T HE SUNLIGHT FELT WONDERFUL ON MY FACE. THE HUGE window in Xavier's room revealed a beautiful blue sky sprinkled with fluffy white clouds. I sat up, trying to hide my yawn from my bed partner. But the gorgeous day took a backseat to my pondering. What would today hold, after last night? Where did this leave us now? I turned to check on his sleeping form, only to find the bed empty. The bathroom perhaps?

I slid out of bed and walked to the other side of the room. The restroom door was open and the space empty. I mangled the bed clothing to remove a sheet and wrapped it around myself. I stopped by the guest room, exchanged the sheet for a robe, and then went down the stairs to the kitchen.

"Xavier," I shouted from room to room. No answer.

I turned and ran face first into the chest of a man in a black suit.

He grabbed my arms and pushed me back. "Mademoiselle, excuse me please. I am here to take you to the…airport. Are your bags ready?"

I was at first merely thankful that this driver spoke English, but then came the kick in the chest. Nausea set in.

"Where is Xavier?"

He shrugged.

"When did you talk with the Doctor?"

"This morning."

So fucking stupid. How could I be so naïve? He'd never promised me more than this. *But he told me he loved me.*

I stared at the floor. Swallowed hard and forced back the tears.

"I'll be right back. Let me get my things."

* * *

With Paris in the rearview mirror, I did my best to move on. But the doctor was always on my mind. It was impossible to evade him at work, although I definitely tried. I stopped using the main entrance to avoid seeing the plaque with his name, and dodged meetings that might cause me to work with his products. Thankfully, I finally had the first restful night since my return, nearly eight-weeks earlier. There was no regret. But the heartache was more than I'd thought possible—for my lost love and for his broken life.

Today, just like every other day, I headed to work, only to find myself standing in front of the receptionist's desk on the tenth floor. The question was always on my tongue, but I was unable to spit it out. She had ways to contact him, not to mention Berta was morally flexible. All I had to do was ask her for his contact info and promise a lunch of fine dining and she would give me the means to reach the doctor. But to what end? He obviously didn't want me, or I would have never left, and he certainly would have found me by now. I could only be so angry with him. Most of my loathing I reserved for myself. So fucking stupid.

"Elaine, we've got to stop meeting like this." Berta smiled from behind her desk.

She was bound to notice my strange behavior sooner or

later, but today there was a reason for my presence. I laughed. "I know strange, isn't it? I hadn't seen you in how long, and now I keep ending up here."

"I mean, Ashley in Marketing does know how to order supplies." Supply ordering had been my cover. I had enough pens to write my name around the world.

Another nervous chuckle. "No mooching of staples today. I have a meeting in the conference room around the corner. I'm just a little early." I left out the part about coming early in hope that I could get the doctor's contact info, but that was need to know, and she didn't need to know.

"Oh, you're in that meeting. Good news, they ordered out for lunch. Zaggerilli's instead of cafeteria gruel, lucky you. Make sure you shoot me a message when you're all done, so I can swipe the leftovers. Even Zaggerilli's a couple of hours cold is better than fresh anything from downstairs."

"You got it."

The bell dinged and Sarah from print marketing stepped off the elevator. I gave a slight wave and turned. "Take care, Berta."

I followed Sarah into the room, chose a high-backed leather seat, and pulled my laptop from my bag.

With the projector connected, the other attendees assembled, and small talk with Sarah complete, I began the obligatory meeting procedures—introductions, reading of the agenda, and goals for the meeting.

My audience only consisted of eight people, and most of them I worked with regularly. The mix of men and woman made for an easy job.

"And if you look here. The adherence of patients taking the newest version of Rx 972 was clearly influenced by the socioeconomic status of the patient." I pointed with the laser pointer to the slide on the white screen.

The door to the room opened and my heart stopped. The man dressed in an expensive black business suit moved into the room and stood behind an empty chair.

I stopped. I couldn't speak. His smile was a special kind of torture.

"Oh, pardon me... Ms...?" He waited for me to finish for him.

What kind of game was he playing? These people most likely knew about the fundraiser in Paris. You didn't associate with Dr. Vincent and have it go unnoticed. I wasn't amused. Through gritted teeth I muttered. "Watkins."

"Please excuse my intrusion, Ms. Watkins, but I'm working on a new formulation of this, and I'm curious how the drug administration has impacted adherence."

"It didn't," I snapped.

Sarah, otherwise known as ass-kisser number one, chimed in, "Oh, Doctor. May I call you Doctor? I took notes. And I believe Elaine said that when the drug was administered through self-administered injection, there was a sharp decline in adherence."

He pulled out the chair, sat and turned to Sarah, "Thank you. And you are?" He smiled at her, touched her arm. He fucking touched her arm.

"Hi. I'm Sarah. I've always wanted to meet you, Doctor. You are one of the most brilliant minds of our time."

His gaze drifted from hers to meet my death stare as he said, "And to think, my mind is the weakest of my talents." He smirked.

I was going to kill him. Getting out of that room became my primary goal. Finish the presentation and bolt.

"As I was saying..."

"Dr. Vincent, I'm glad to finally meet you. I'm Mitch. I

worked on the roll out for your last drug when it went to market. It's great to meet you."

The posturing made me want to puke.

"Very nice to meet you, Mitch." The doctor reached across the table and shook his hand. "But I'm sure Ms. Watkins has another meeting after this, so let's let her finish. We can catch up later."

"As I was saying, the socioeconomic status of the patient impacts the level of adherence."

"Excuse me, Ms. Watkins. Did you receive the Parisian study that I sent your department head?"

Parisian study? Was he fucking kidding? I tried not to let my irritation show. It was one thing if he wanted to pretend our week together never happened, but I wished he had the decency to disappear. Why was he doing this?

He raised an eyebrow, and from the expression on my co-workers faces, I'd paused for far too long. Leading me before to believe he cared was almost excusable, but this… After all, an agreement was an agreement. I'd spent the last eight weeks chalking it up to clever role-playing. This was outright cruel.

"No, I was told the Parisian study was top secret, and findings were never to be released."

"You are correct, Ms. Watkins. But there are certain elements I was able to have declassified to support your research. Did you receive it? I asked Berta to deliver it to your office this morning."

I gripped the laser pointer. "I'm quite certain I didn't receive anything."

He stood. "You know what? We could probably all use a break. Why don't we adjourn until the top of the hour and you can go check?"

I opened my mouth to object, but before the words could leave, he said, "Thanks everyone," and waved his hand toward the door urging them out.

With everyone gone we both stood there. Him staring at his clasped hands and me waiting for him to come clean.

He looked up. "Ms. Watkins, we don't have all day. They will be back soon."

Disbelief. I couldn't believe he continued the act. I slammed the laser pointer onto the conference room table and stormed out.

I didn't bother with the elevator; five flights of stairs would help burn off some of the frustration. How could he justify taunting me, especially after rejecting me?

I threw open the stairway door and marched down the hallway. There was no fucking report. I felt bad for what had happened to him, but this wasn't funny.

Most of the people on the floor had left for lunch. I walked into my dark office, not bothering even to turn light on, because the good doctor was full of shit.

I picked up several interoffice envelopes from my inbox. None of them seemed heavy enough to hold a report, but I began the laborious task of unwinding the red string that secured each envelope's contents. First one: signed expense reports. This was a complete waste of time.

The slam of the door closing and click of the lock caused me to drop the packet.

Xavier Vincent stood, adjusting his cufflinks.

"What do you want?"

"I want you to continue to look for that report."

I brushed my hair out of my face. "Fine. You still want to play games."

I bent down to pick up the envelopes.

When I stood up his body pinned me to the front of the desk. My thighs rested against the mahogany woodwork that decorated the edge of the work surface.

He wound his arms around me, reaching under my breast and up to grasp my chin. Oh God, the feel of him, his scorching body against my back, cock hard and breath hot on my neck. "You left."

Air was in short supply. The effect he had on me couldn't be denied. Relief that we were done pretending flooded through at the same time as dread.

His finger stroked my cheek.

"Yes. I can take a hint. The driver said you called him that morning. Besides, you made it clear."

He gripped me a little tighter. "Did I? What exactly was clear to you, Elaine?" His voice was rough as he growled the words.

"One week. That's all. You stay in your world, and I go back to mine. Wasn't that the agreement?"

His hand grasped my breast and squeezed. "Yes, but I was pretty certain we amended that agreement when I told you I loved you."

I was suddenly glad that I wasn't facing him. Tears pricked at the corners of my eyes. That was the scene I relived every night, followed by the driver asking me if my bags were ready. I swallowed hard, trying not to cry.

"I did call the driver. After I called and arranged to have the seat beside you on the flight back. I planned to come with you."

Oh God. The seat beside me in first class had been empty.

"I left for my morning jog and when I returned you were gone." He squeezed my chin. "My life had fallen apart, and the one thing I needed most left me."

Now I was angry. Why did he take so long to tell me? I had been miserable. He could have found me at any time.

"I didn't leave you. If I had known, I would have stayed."

"What did you think I was doing? Pretending?"

Tears escaped, rolled down my cheeks, and pooled between my face and his fingers. There was no hiding it now. "Role-playing. I thought it was part of the game. What took you so long to tell me?"

"Was your reaction to me a game? A role you were playing?"

"Of course not."

He sighed. "I was on my way to the airport. I had every intention of tracking you down, when Sebastian called. Miriam killed herself."

"Oh no."

"Her note to you was her final atonement. But that meant two things. I had a friend to console, and any hope of getting answers to my fucked up past were gone."

"I'm so sorry."

"Sebastian was prepared to lose her to the disease, but he couldn't handle her decision when she still had life in her."

I gripped him and stroked his arm through the fabric of his jacket.

"The more time that passed, the more I convinced myself that perhaps it was for the best. As I helped Sebastian with his grief, my own changed." He placed a soft kiss to my neck. "I poured through the documents in Lydia's office and grew angrier and angrier. Did you know that my name isn't Xavier Vincent? I was patient X in something called the Veritas Project. When I was placed with the original people I thought were my parents, it was the name I was given."

"Oh my God."

"I'm the result of an experiment. A secret society of psychiatric professionals, who think it's their right to mind fuck people at their whim, for whatever perversion they have. They are rich and virtually unstoppable."

"So are you."

He paused. He kissed my neck, nipping slightly with his teeth. "This is why I love you. But you have to understand, I don't know who I am. Xavier Vincent lab rat doesn't exist anymore. I answer to no one. I'm going to hunt them down one by one and expose them." His lips played across the divot at the base my throat.

My heart raced, ached and swelled. His love wasn't imaginary, but his pain was more than even I had the capacity to understand.

He sucked in a deep breath. "Remember how we made rain in the gallery?"

I swallowed hard. How could I forget? "Yes."

"There was one part of the story I left out. The king, after watching his wife be ravished, and made to come repeatedly for hours on end by the town's men, stands up from his throne, and with the townspeople gathered around, he is the final one to take his wife."

His hand moved from my breast and began scooting my skirt up my thighs. "They believed the last man to take her would be the father of any children produced, so there were never any bastard children. Have you been with anyone else since me?"

"Are you kidding? No, I haven't been able to think straight, let alone think about dating."

"Good."

"What if I had said yes?"

"I'd demand it never happen again. Your king is here to

take back what belongs to him." With both hands he worked my skirt up my thighs, bunching it around my waist. "This will be most poetic." He wrapped his arm around my waist, bent me forward, sliding his fingers inside my panties and between my folds.

"What do you mean?" I groaned as he began stroking my clit.

"You see the king knows his queen's body better than anyone else, and in front of all of the town's people he makes her come one last time. He fucks her with everyone standing witness. He is the last to spill his seed inside her and in the process he ends his sacrifice." He rubbed harder, and on the down stroke his fingers entered me. "I am ready to reclaim you. We'd both be fired if I fucked you on the conference room table in the meeting, so here's the plan."

He increased his rhythm. His other hand slipped inside my shirt and teased my nipple, while he pressed his hard cock tight against my ass.

"I'm going to make you come, and then I'm going to come inside you. We're going to go back to that meeting together, and there will be no doubt in their minds what happened. I'm going to make sure you are well fucked before you return."

"But aren't you worried about what people will think?"

He buried his fingers deep. "Yes, I'm worried one of them might not know that you belong to me. This pussy is mine. For my entire life everyone else has made the rules for me. I'm taking back control and I'm starting with you." He kissed up my neck to my earlobe and I moaned. "Even if you had said you'd left on purpose, you weren't getting away. I'm not a victim anymore, Elaine. I'm your king. I will conquer you. Possess you to make sure that when I finally find who I really am, there's something to ground me in who I wanted to be."

The harder and faster his fingers moved, the slicker I

became. "Come for me, my queen. Let them all know who you belong to."

He sucked hard on my neck and his pelvis thrust against my ass. Rapid thrusts in and out of me, his thumb moved to my clit rubbing in time with his penetrating fingers.

I threw my head back against his shoulder as euphoria flooded my mind.

"Oh, Xavier. Fuck. I'm gonna come."

"Now, do it now."

He turned my head to the side and captured my lips. His tongue slid into my mouth as his fingers fucked me hard. He swallowed my moan and I shook with ecstasy.

A few more strokes over my wet core and his hand disappeared. The distinct sound of a lowering zipper filled the room.

His cock's head touched my thighs and he pushed me forward on the desk.

His hands moved between my legs and widened my stance. He nudged at my entrance, placed his hands on my hips and pulled me back, burying his cock to the hilt.

"Fuck. You feel so good. Even better than I remembered."

He started with a steady rhythm and moaned with each thrust.

"I love you, Elaine. I hope you can love who I become."

Big thrust. He wrapped his fist in my hair, stealing the words from my lips.

"Because, Elaine, I need you to be my constant. To tame the beast that's out for vengeance. To be the one thing I can depend on. You told me the truth when walking away would have been easier. With you I'll find that piece of me that I'm afraid I'll lose in all this rage."

Harder and harder he pounded. I shifted my hips giving

him deeper access and his balls slapped against my swollen clit.

"Fuck," he gasped as I came again. Squeezing him, making me feel deliciously full. He was a large man and the new tightness spurred him on.

"You're so tight. I can't get enough. God...so fucking good."

I gripped the desk and held on while he slammed into me, wet flesh slapping against wet flesh.

"I'm going to come, Elaine. I'm taking back my queen." A deep thrust. "Fuck."

Sharp, deep thrust followed by warmth and more fullness.

He leaned forward and placed a kiss on the back of my neck. Between heavy breaths he whispered, "I love you, Elaine. Nothing will ever change that."

The sound of laughter drifted in from the elevators as people returned from lunch.

I tried to stand up. Before I could, he pulled out and spun me around to face him. He sat me on the edge of the desk and reached between my legs and pulled my panties back into place and ran his fingers over them, moistening them with the evidence of our lovemaking.

"Just in case you decide to freshen up."

"Don't you trust me?"

He cupped my face. I breathed deeply; our combined scent, heady. "You are the only thing I trust. The question is, can you trust me enough to let me love you like I need to now? I need your surrender."

"I surrender, because I love you, my king." He stared deep into my eyes, searching for something, and after a moment responded with a kiss more passionate than any before.

As he released my lips, he tucked himself in, zipped up. He helped me off the desk to stand and smoothed down my skirt.

"Let's go present my queen."

I laughed. "They're going to think I slept with you to get you off my back about the presentation."

A quick kiss. "You needn't worry. In my kingdom, you and I will rule as equals. Only in my chambers will you submit. They will have no doubt that what you did was not a favor. Besides, I made all of that up, there was no report. I'm fully prepared to tell them about how you put me in my place. Does it bother you that I just had my way with you in your office? Afraid they'll accuse you of fucking the boss?"

"Well...I do have to continue working here after you get bored."

"What?" His eyes narrowed, and turned cold as steel.

"I mean... I just..." I stared past him at the floor.

He placed his hands on either side of my face. "Look here." He forced me to meet his gaze. "This isn't some passing fancy. You've consumed my every thought since you left Paris. Even those thoughts you shouldn't have." He tightened his grip on my face. "I'm standing on the precipice of hell, knowing I have to jump. And even though it's wrong of me, I want you with me. If you want me to tell them that, I will."

"No," I said, feeling stupid for my moment of doubt.

"Besides, we'll both need to take a leave of absence to hunt down these bastards."

"But the other cure...my job..."

"Please understand, until this is sorted out, I can't clear my head enough to work on it."

How could I blame him? After my dad's discovery, I was pretty much worthless. "Fair enough. But my job...and how are you going to explain this?" I traced the line of his lip.

He reached up and pulled the birdcage necklace from my shirt and held it up for me to see.

"Your job will be here for you when we're done. That's if you still want it. You might find being queen a more fitting position." He smiled. "As for us…you freed me. I won't let them put you in a cage. I love you, Elaine. That's what I'll tell them. I just hope that you can learn to love me, because Xavier Vincent was an illusion."

"What makes you think I haven't seen the real you from the beginning?"

He raised my hand to his lips placing a soft kiss. "Maybe you have and that's why I had to have you. Now if you can survive the truth…"

"At least in truth there is no pain, because it can't be undone. People are wrong, when they talk of the painful truth. It's not the birth of the truth that causes the most agony; it's the death of the lie that leaves us crippled. And most excruciating are those false truths we weave for ourselves. Lies unravel, painful stitch by stitch. In truth, Doctor, you'll find the cure for every lie."

"And for me that cure is you."

# ~ Coming Soon ~

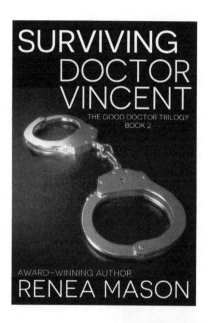

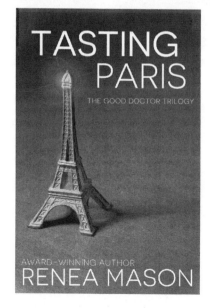

# ~ AVAILABLE ON AUDIO BOOK ~

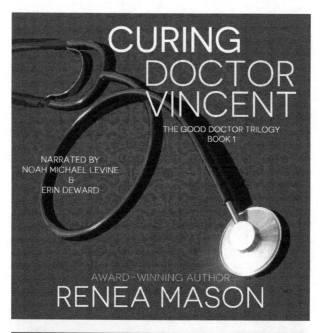

CURING DOCTOR VINCENT

THE GOOD DOCTOR TRILOGY
BOOK 1

NARRATED BY
NOAH MICHAEL LEVINE
&
ERIN DEWARD

AWARD-WINNING AUTHOR
RENEA MASON

SYMPHONY OF LIGHT SERIES ~ BOOK 1 ~

Narrated by
Erin deWard
and
Noah Michael
Levine

SYMPHONY
of
LIGHT and WINTER

BESTSELLING AND AWARD-WINNING AUTHOR
RENEA MASON

Bonus Material ~ *Impostors' Kiss* ~ Prequel to *Symphony of Light and Winter*

# ~ ABOUT THE AUTHOR ~

Renea Mason, author of the award-winning novel, *Symphony of Light and Winter*, writes erotic paranormal and contemporary romance.

When she isn't putting pen to paper, crafting sensual stories filled with supernatural and larger-than-life lovers, she spends time with her beyond-supportive husband, two wonderful sons and two loving but needy cats.

Renea loves connecting with her readers. Visit her on…

Website
http://ReneaMason.com

Facebook
http://www.facebook.com/ReneaMasonAuthor

Twitter @reneamason1
https://twitter.com/ReneaMason1

Fan Club
http://www.facebook.com/groups/TheMadMasons

# ~ OTHER BOOKS BY RENEA MASON ~

## SYMPHONY OF LIGHT AND WINTER
### SYMPHONY OF LIGHT, BOOK #1

Award-winning debut novel by Renea Mason
- 2nd place for Erotica/Romantica for Write Touch Award Contest sponsored by the Wisconsin Romance Writers – Romance Writers of America Chapter
- 3rd place award for Best New Paranormal Romance of 2013 in The Paranormal Romance Guild's Reviewers Choice Awards
- Finalist in the Paranormal category for the Passionate Plume Contest sponsored by the special interest chapter of the Romance Writers of America – Passionate Ink
- Finalist for Best First Book in the National Excellence in Romance Fiction Award sponsored by the First Coast Romance Writers – Romance Writers of America Chapter
- Finalist in the Heart of Denver Romance Writers of America Chapter's Heart Aspen Gold Contest for Paranormal Romances

*One woman. Seven men. All bound by one man's undying devotion.*

Ten years after watching life drain from her former mentor and first love's eyes, Linden Hill's skills for divining the predictable are lost. When Cyril returns, he's still gorgeous, but this time he's beyond human, far less dead, and pissed.

His lack of memory drives him to desperate acts, and his turbulent re-acquaintance with Linden pulls her into his war with a creature hell-bent on his destruction. His group of six supernatural men share a tantalizing secret, but despite the hunger, it's love that leads her to sacrifice everything to save him...

## IMPOSTORS' KISS
### SYMPHONY OF LIGHT, #0.5 PREQUEL

In a night of passion, two lost spirits find solace in an impostor's kiss: one longing for a love that doesn't yet exist, the other drowning in pain and guilt over love lost. Neither is what they seem...but what they learn will change them forever...

## BETWEEN THE WATERS
### SYMPHONY OF LIGHT, BOOK #2

*Magic is no match for love...*

Trapped somewhere between life and death, demigod Cyril has lost the ability to communicate with his love. But not before giving her valuable lessons in magic, as well as his blessing to move on without him.

Coming to terms with Cyril's absence isn't easy, but Linden is doing her best to honor his wishes, until she receives an unusual request from Moreaux, an estranged member of Cyril's family. Bizarre things are going on with Mary, the former housekeeper, and Linden can't let them go. But when her investigation leads to a mistake that nearly costs her life, Cyril's best friend, Overton, steps in and violates a promise he made centuries before to bring her back from the dead.

Gratitude turns to comfort, comfort turns to desire, and desire leads Linden to a shocking revelation. In her charge to uncover the truth behind Mary and Moreaux, she discovers a spell she can't undo without leaving wounds on her heart, wounds she knows will never heal...

http://reneamason.com

23915426R00131

Made in the USA
Middletown, DE
07 September 2015